**"There are too many puzzle pieces,"
she said. "In the meantime, you and
I—maybe Cora, too—are in the crosshairs
of a killer."**

Eli didn't argue with her. Couldn't. Because it was
true, a frustration that they both felt. That frustration
was in every muscle of his body when he pulled
her into his arms. As he'd done in the kitchen, he
brushed a kiss on the top of her head. A kiss of
comfort.

And it worked.

Ashlyn could practically feel some of the tension
slide right out of her. Of course, the heat came in its
place. No surprise there. She'd been dealing with it
for much too long.

He pulled back just a little and looked down at her
with those smoky gray eyes. They weren't stormy
now but had some of the same fire that she was
certain were in her own.

"Yeah," he said, as if he'd known exactly what she
was thinking—and feeling.

SETTLING AN
OLD SCORE

***

USA TODAY Bestselling Author
DELORES FOSSEN

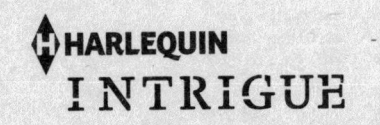

HARLEQUIN®
INTRIGUE®

Recycling programs for this product may not exist in your area.

ISBN-13: 978-1-335-13663-3

Settling an Old Score

Harlequin Enterprises ULC
22 Adelaide St. West, 40th Floor
Toronto, Ontario M5H 4E3, Canada
www.Harlequin.com

Printed in U.S.A.

Delores Fossen, a *USA TODAY* bestselling author, has written over one hundred novels, with millions of copies of her books in print worldwide. She's received a Booksellers' Best Award and an RT Reviewers' Choice Best Book Award. She was also a finalist for a prestigious RITA® Award. You can contact the author through her website at www.deloresfossen.com.

Books by Delores Fossen

Harlequin Intrigue

Longview Ridge Ranch

Safety Breach
A Threat to His Family
Settling an Old Score

**The Lawmen of
McCall Canyon**

Cowboy Above the Law
Finger on the Trigger
Lawman with a Cause
Under the Cowboy's Protection

Blue River Ranch

Always a Lawman
Gunfire on the Ranch
Lawman from Her Past
Roughshod Justice

HQN Books

Lone Star Ridge

Tangled Up in Texas
That Night in Texas
(ebook novella)
Chasing Trouble in Texas

A Coldwater Texas Novel

Lone Star Christmas
Lone Star Midnight
(ebook novella)
Hot Texas Sunrise
Texas at Dusk
(ebook novella)
Sweet Summer Sunset
A Coldwater Christmas

Visit the Author Profile page at Harlequin.com.

CAST OF CHARACTERS

Texas Ranger Eli Slater—This cowboy lawman won't let anything, including bad blood, get in the way of protecting his old flame and her newborn daughter.

Ashlyn Darrow—Once, she loved Eli, and even though there's an old score to settle between them, she has no choice but to turn to him when a kidnapper comes after her baby.

Cora Darrow—Ashlyn's adopted daughter, who's caught up in the danger when Ashlyn and Eli are attacked.

Dominick McComb—Cora's biological grandfather. He would do anything to get custody of her.

Leon Taggart—Even though he's in jail, could he be the one who's continuing the reign of violence against Eli and Ashlyn?

Remy Sager—He could have crossed the line while seeking revenge for the death of his lover, and that might have made Eli and Ashlyn targets.

Oscar Cronin—A shady businessman who might be looking for payback for the arrest of his old friend Leon Taggart.

Chapter One

The sound woke Texas Ranger Eli Slater. Something, or *someone*, was on his front porch.

He'd heard footsteps, maybe. Or maybe it was just some animal on a nighttime prowl. Since he lived in the country, something like that was always a possibility.

When he heard another sound, he checked the clock on the nightstand. It was just after midnight. And he cursed because there was no way he would get back to sleep unless he made sure this wasn't a would-be burglar. If that was the case, it'd be a stupid one since the fool was at the house of a Texas Ranger. A heavily armed and grouchy Ranger, since Eli had just finished a long shift only a couple of hours earlier.

He threw back the covers and first glanced at his phone to make sure that he hadn't missed a text from his family. He had three brothers, and since all of them were lawmen, there was a chance that there could be some kind of emergency. But there were no texts or missed calls.

That put a knot in his stomach.

He was glad there was no family crisis, but that could have been a reasonable explanation for why someone was visiting him at this god-awful hour. So, if it wasn't family, then who was it?

He cursed again when he heard the sound for the third time. Definitely footsteps, and not those of an animal. Eli dragged on his jeans, slipped his phone into his pocket and grabbed the SIG Sauer he kept next to his bed. He hoped this would be a quick check that would turn out to be nothing. Maybe a neighbor with car trouble. Then he could deal with it, get right back in bed and hope that he didn't dream about…anything.

Especially *her.*

But hoping hadn't ever helped him much in that department. She made regular appearances in his nightmares. That was his punishment, he supposed. A woman was dead because of him, and Eli figured even a couple of lifetimes wouldn't be enough to help him come to terms with that.

"Who's out there?" Eli shouted when he made it to the living room.

The footsteps on the porch came again, and this time the person was running. Maybe that meant this was possibly some kind of prank from local teenagers.

Since it was July, school was out, and his ranch was just a stone's throw off the road leading into town. It could be that some kids had too much time on their hands. If so, Eli was in an ornery enough mood to arrest their sorry butts for waking him up. Then he'd take them into Longview Ridge to the sheriff's office where his brother, the sheriff, could put them in jail for a few hours.

"Just in case you're too stupid not to know this—I'm Sergeant Eli Slater, Texas Ranger," he added.

No more footsteps, but he did hear something else. A strange mewing sound. Maybe a kitten? Oh, man. Had the pranking clowns left a stray cat on his porch?

Eli went to the door, keeping to the side of it while he opened it, and he peered out into the darkness. Nothing. Until he looked down.

What the hell?

It was a car seat, and there was a thin blanket draped over it. At first glimpse Eli thought maybe the cat was inside it, but then the blanket moved, and he saw the foot.

A baby's foot.

That put his heart right in his throat, and he fired glances all around the yard to see who'd done this. No one was in sight.

The baby whimpered, kicking at the blanket, and while Eli still kept watch of the yard, he stooped down for a better look. That look got a whole lot easier for him when the baby's kicking caused the blanket to slide off the car seat.

Yeah, it was a baby all right, and not some automated doll as he'd hoped.

A baby dressed in a pink gown. He wasn't an expert on kids by any means, but he thought that maybe the baby was a couple of months old. And he or she wasn't very happy, with that bottom lip poked out, and staring up at him as if about to start crying at any second.

"If this is a joke, I don't find it funny," Eli called out to the person who'd left the baby.

But a joke didn't feel right. This went well beyond something that bored kids would do. Had someone actually abandoned the baby on his porch? His place wasn't a "safe haven" for leaving unwanted infants; that was usually reserved for fire stations and police departments. But it could have happened.

Still keeping watch in case someone was out there, Eli checked to make sure the little one was okay. There wasn't a scratch on the baby that he could see, and he or she appeared to be clean. That was something, at least. And whoever had left the baby had tucked a bottle into the side of the seat. So someone had been feeding the kid.

"Who did this?" Eli shouted, trying again to get some kind of response from the person responsible for the baby.

But nothing. Well, nothing other than the baby,

who started to whimper. Hell. That caused the adrenaline to spike through him, and while he took out his phone, he rocked the car seat a little, hoping it would soothe the child. It didn't. The whimpering turned into a full-fledged cry.

He scrolled through his contacts to his brother Kellan, the sheriff, but before Eli could even press the number, he saw a slash of headlights as a vehicle turned off the main road and started toward his place.

Fast.

The car sped right at him, skidding to a stop in front of his house. His first thought was this was someone who was about to clear up the situation. Maybe someone frantic. A blond-haired woman wearing a gauzy white dress bolted from the car. She was armed, and she aimed the gun that she whipped up right at him.

And he groaned.

Because he knew his visitor—Ashlyn Darrow. As a lawman, he'd made enemies, had dealt with his share of bad blood, and Ashlyn was at the top of the bad blood list. In her mind she thought he was the bad guy.

He wasn't.

But Eli doubted he would convince her of that—ever. Especially after what'd happened.

Despite him trying to push it away, pieces of the repeating nightmare came. Ashlyn was in that nightmare, but like now she was very much alive. The other woman wasn't.

"Get away from her," Ashlyn ordered.

If Eli had had on his badge, he would have tapped it to give her a reminder that she didn't need. Ashlyn knew full well that he was a Ranger, and she had no badge and no right, legal or otherwise, to pull a gun on him. Still, he had no intention of trading shots with her, not with the baby right at his feet. Just in case Ashlyn pulled the trigger, though, he moved in front of the little girl. He seriously doubted she would do something like that if she knew there was a baby involved.

"Put down your gun," he warned her. "Along with pissing me off, you're endangering a child."

A burst of air left her mouth. It was a humorless laugh. "You've already endangered her. Just like you did Marta."

There it came again. Bits of the nightmares, and it always sickened him that the pieces could be just as potent as the real thing. Two years hadn't toned down the bits, either, and despite the bad blood between Ashlyn and him, Eli thought maybe it was the same for her.

Since talking about Marta Seaver wasn't going to help this situation, Eli went with a question that would hopefully give him the start of the answers he needed. "Put down your gun and tell me what you know about this baby. Were you the one who left her here?"

Even though it was dark, there was enough light coming from the porch that he saw the confusion go through her eyes. Brown eyes, he knew. And he knew them well. Or rather *had known* them.

She shook her head, lowering her gun just a little, but then he saw another emotion. Pure anger. "You know how the baby got here, because you were the one to take her," she insisted.

Now he was the one who was no doubt showing some confusion. "I was in bed asleep." He tipped his head to his lack of shirt and boots. "I heard a noise, came to the porch to check it out, and she was here. A couple of minutes later, you showed up with a gun."

Ashlyn stared at him, repeated the headshake, and she started moving closer. Eli didn't think he was the reason for that, though. The baby started fussing.

"Is she hurt?" Ashlyn asked, her thick breath gusting.

"She seems fine to me, but I didn't pick her up for a closer look. I was about to call Kellan, and then I would have taken her to the hospital just to be sure."

If Ashlyn heard any of that, it didn't register on her face. As the baby's fussing got louder, Ashlyn moved faster. She practically barreled up the steps, and the moment that she reached him, Eli stripped the gun from her hand.

She made a strangled sound of fear and frustration, but she didn't fight to get the weapon back. Instead, Ashlyn dropped to her knees and picked up the baby, pulling the infant right against her.

"She's okay," Ashlyn said, raw relief in her voice, and she just kept repeating it.

He'd known Ashlyn since they were kids, but it'd been two years since he'd seen her. Not since that night of Marta's death and the shooting that'd nearly ended Ashlyn's life, too. She hadn't actually cried that night, had been more in shock and then too drugged up on the pain meds for her injuries. However, she was crying now, and the tears were streaming down her face.

Eli wasn't immune to those tears, either. Ashlyn's grief already felt like a fist around his heart, and that fist was squeezing hard now.

He tucked both of their guns in the back waist of his jeans and glanced out at her car to make sure no one else was inside. If there was, he didn't see them.

"Whose baby is this? Is she yours?" he demanded, and he made sure his lawman's tone came through loud and clear.

But his tone faltered a bit when he recalled something. Yet more memories of the attack two years ago. Ashlyn had been shot three times, and the bullets had done a lot of damage. Eli was pretty sure he remembered the doctors saying that she'd never be able to have a child.

An injury like that was something that only added to his nightmares. One woman was dead and the other wounded to the point that it had changed her life forever and taken away her chance to become a mother. A biological one, anyway.

"She's mine. Her name is Cora, and I adopted her," Ashlyn added as if she'd known he was thinking about the shooting.

Eli hadn't heard about the adoption, but then Ashlyn wasn't exactly a frequent visitor to Longview Ridge. Probably because she hadn't wanted to risk running into him. By avoiding him, she'd also avoided the inevitable gossip that came with living in a small town.

"If you didn't bring Cora here, then who did?" he asked.

Ashlyn still had tears in her eyes when she looked up at him. She opened her mouth, closed it and shook her head for a third time. She glanced away from him as if trying to figure out how to answer, and with the baby gripped in her arms, she quickly stood.

"Oh God," she blurted out. "They could be watching us. They could still hurt her."

That got his attention, and even though Eli still didn't have all the answers he wanted, he hurried Ashlyn inside his house and shut the door. Eli immediately started to pat Ashlyn down, working his hands around the baby.

Ashlyn made a sound of outrage. One that Eli ignored.

"You showed up here out of the blue and pulled a gun on me," he grumbled. "Just in case you're carrying our bad blood to the next level, I don't want you trying to kill me."

She didn't exactly jump to defend herself or claim that killing him had never been on her agenda. That didn't ease the tight muscles in his chest.

"I would have done anything to get her back." Ashlyn's voice trembled as she kissed the baby again. But then she froze for a moment before she looked up at him. "And they knew that. Oh God. They knew that."

"They?" Eli challenged. Once he was certain she wasn't armed, he engaged the security system and looked out the side window of the front door.

"The men who took Cora." Her breath shuddered, and she started to sob again.

Eli didn't have a stone heart, so that got to him. So did the fact that an innocent little baby was somehow involved in this. Whatever *this* was.

"Keep talking," he insisted while he continued to keep watch. Ashlyn had left on her car headlights so that helped him see the road that led to his house. "Tell me what happened." And then he would almost certainly need to call Kellan. First, though,

Eli wanted to hear the specifics so he'd know what to relay to his brother.

"I was in bed at my house. Cora was asleep in the nursery." Ashlyn's voice got shakier with each word. So did she. Whatever had happened had spooked her, and he was positive that she wasn't faking it. "Two men broke down the door. Cops," she spat out, aiming a glare at him. A glare that quickly softened as if she'd heard what she'd said and realized it didn't ring true.

"Two cops broke into your house?" He didn't bother to take out the skepticism. "Did they have a warrant? Did they ID themselves?"

Ashlyn shook her head. "They were wearing uniforms, badges and all the gear that cops have. They used a stun gun on me." She rubbed her fingers along the side of her arm, and the trembling got worse. "They took Cora, but I heard them say they were working for you."

Eli's groan was even louder than she one she made. "And you believed them." The look he gave her was as flat as his tone. He didn't spell out to her that she'd been gullible, but he was certain Ashlyn had already picked up on that.

She squeezed her eyes shut a moment. "I panicked. Wasn't thinking straight. As soon as I could move, I jumped in my car and drove straight here."

The drive wouldn't have taken that long since Ashlyn's house was only about ten miles away. She lived on a small ranch on the other side of Longview Ridge that she'd inherited from her grandparents, and she made a living training and boarding horses.

"Did the kidnappers make a ransom demand?" he pressed. "Or did they take anything else from your place?"

"No. They only took Cora. Who brought her here?" Ashlyn asked, her head whipping up. "Was it those cops?"

"*Fake* cops," Eli automatically corrected. "I didn't see who left her on my porch, but they weren't exactly quiet about it. She was probably out here no more than a minute or two before I went to the door and found her."

He paused, worked through the pieces that she'd just given him, and it didn't take him long to come to a conclusion. A bad one. These fake cops hadn't hurt the child, hadn't asked for money or taken anything, but they had let Ashlyn believe they worked for him. There had to be a good reason for that. Well, "good" in their minds, anyway.

"This was some kind of sick game?" she asked.

It was looking that way. A game designed to send her after him.

"They wanted me to kill you?" Ashlyn added a moment later.

Before Eli answered that, he wanted to talk to his brother and get backup so he could take Ashlyn and the baby into Longview Ridge. First to the hospital to confirm they were okay and then to the sheriff's office so he could get an official statement from Ashlyn.

"You really had no part in this?" she pressed.

Eli huffed, not bothering to answer that. He took out his phone to make that call to Kellan, but he stopped when he saw the blur of motion on the other side of Ashlyn's car. He lifted his hand to silence her when Ashlyn started to speak, and he kept looking.

Waiting.

Then, he finally saw it. Or rather he saw *them*. Two men wearing uniforms, and they had guns aimed right at the house.

Chapter Two

Ashlyn immediately noticed the change in Eli's body language, and she heard the single word of profanity that he said under his breath. And she knew something else was horribly wrong.

"Did those cops come back? Those *men*?" she corrected.

Not cops. Now that she had her baby safe in her arms and was seeing things a little clearer, she knew that. Well, unless they were dirty lawmen, but she doubted they would have shown up in uniform and full gear if they had been.

"Someone's out there," Eli confirmed, and while volleying his attention between the window and his phone, he fired off a text to someone. Kellan, no doubt. "Get down and stay down," he added as he finished the text.

Ashlyn held Cora close to her while she hurried to the sofa and dropped down on the side of it. "How good is your security system?" she asked, trying to tamp down the fear that was racing through her.

"Good," Eli verified. "But yours would have been, too, and yet they still managed to get in."

That only caused her heart to pound even harder. Because he was right. After she'd nearly been killed two years ago, after Marta had died, Ashlyn had added a security system with motion detectors, but no alarms had gone off when the men had broken in.

She groaned. "They jammed it." Eli didn't verify that, didn't need to. It was the only thing that made sense. Actually, it was one of the few things that actually made sense. They'd jammed it so they could get to her before she could grab a weapon or try to defend herself. But why had they set her up to go after Eli?

If that's what had actually happened.

"The men aren't coming closer," Eli told her. "They're behind the trees across the road from your car. As soon as Kellan gets here, I'll go out there and confront them."

She was shaking her head before he even finished. "If you go out there, they could gun you down."

"Maybe. But they would have had a chance to do that when I stepped on the porch and found the baby. And they could have killed you when they broke into your house or even after you arrived here."

That robbed Ashlyn of what little breath she'd managed to gather. Mercy, he was right. They could have shot her instead of using the stun gun. Once they'd overpowered her, they could have done whatever they'd wanted.

"What's going on?" she mumbled.

"The hell if I know, but trust me when I say this, I will find out."

Eli glanced back at her again, and even though the lights in the room were off, she could see his intense expression. Of course, plenty of things were intense about Eli. He was the tough Slater brother, the hard-nosed Texas Ranger who could intimidate with a single look.

Like now.

Of course, the intimidation was lessened some by the fact he was bare to the waist and his jeans weren't even zipped. For just a split second, before she could push it away, Ashlyn saw the hot cowboy that she'd once crushed on way back in high school.

"You'd better not be lying to me about any of this," he snarled.

And just like that, he caused the "crush" thoughts to vanish in a flash. "Everything that I've told you is the truth."

It was. But with their history, she couldn't blame him for asking. However, she could perhaps blame him for what'd gone on.

"If these men wanted me to kill you, then maybe it's because of a case you're working on. Maybe it's because of Marta," she added.

Ashlyn waited for the glare that she was certain he would send her way, but there wasn't one. Maybe because he got an interruption when his phone rang. He put the call on speaker while he continued to keep watch, and it didn't take long before she heard the familiar voice.

Sheriff Kellan Slater.

"I'm just up the road, and I have the two men in sight," Kellan explained. "You're right. They're armed. From what I can see both have handguns, and one has a rifle with a scope."

Eli's scowl deepened, and she thought she knew why. The handguns might not be much of a threat to them if the men stayed across the road because of the range of the bullets, but they could use the rifle to fire into the house. If that's what they planned, that is. But as Eli had pointed out, they hadn't shot at either him or her when they'd had a chance.

"Gunnar's on the way," Kellan added a moment later. "I'd like to hold off doing anything until he gets here, and he can block the road from the other end."

Gunnar was Deputy Gunnar Pullam, whom Ashlyn had known most of her life. Like Kellan, he didn't live too far away, which hopefully meant he'd be there soon. That way, if they could pen in the men, they might be able to catch and then question them.

"You have IDs on these two?" Kellan asked Eli.

"No. But I believe they might have brought Ashlyn's adopted baby to my house and left her on my doorstep."

"What?" Kellan sounded just as stunned as Eli had been when she'd first shown up.

"Yeah," was all Eli said. "I need to grab my boots from my bedroom," he added to Kellan. "If we have to chase these guys, I don't want to be barefoot. Ashlyn is on the floor, and she'll stay down."

"I'll keep watch," Kellan assured him. "Hurry."

The urgency in Kellan's voice came through loud and clear, and it gave Ashlyn another jolt of adrenaline that she didn't need. At least Cora had stopped fussing and had fallen back asleep. That hopefully meant the baby wasn't picking up on the terror that Ashlyn was feeling.

Eli ran back to his bedroom, and within seconds he returned with his boots, holster and shirt. He laid his phone on the small table next to the door while he put them on and continued to volley glances out the window.

It didn't take Eli long to dress, and when he put on the shirt, she saw his badge was already attached, and just like that the memories washed over her like a tidal wave. He'd been wearing the badge the night of the shooting. She could feel and smell the air in the parking lot of the seedy bar where Marta had asked Ashlyn to meet her. It'd been thick, humid. Smothering.

Ashlyn could also feel the bullets slam into her.

She felt the cold shock that followed. Then, the pain. Especially the pain. It hadn't been just physical, either, after she'd seen Marta, her best friend, lying in a pool of her own blood.

Dead.

So was the person who'd fired those shots, Drake Zeller, a drug dealer scumbag whom Eli had managed to take out. But not before Zeller had put three bullets into Ashlyn and a fatal one into Marta. The only person who was still standing, still unharmed, after the gunfight was Eli—and he was the reason Zeller had been after Marta. Ashlyn had simply been collateral damage.

"Gunnar will have the road blocked in about five minutes," she heard Kellan relay to Eli, but then the sheriff cursed. "Wait. The men are on the move."

That pushed away the thoughts of that horrible night, and Ashlyn automatically tightened her grip on the baby. She considered asking Eli if she could have her gun back, but she didn't want it that close to Cora.

"Hell," Eli spat out as he ran out of the foyer and into the living room, very close to the sofa where Ashlyn was. He took up position at the window, which would give him a different angle to the front yard and the road.

"Are they getting away?" she asked.

"Can't tell yet. They're no longer in sight, but they could have just dropped back."

And with that rifle, they'd still be a threat. Maybe, though, Gunnar would have had time to finish that roadblock.

Eli's phone dinged, and his forehead bunched up when he looked down at the screen. "I've got another call with a blocked number." He paused. "It could be these thugs. I'll put you on hold while I find out."

While volleying glances at the window, Eli switched over the call, but he didn't say anything. He just waited, and several seconds later, she heard the man who came onto the line.

"Still alive, Sergeant Slater?" the caller asked.

Ashlyn gasped because she recognized that voice, too. Unlike Kellan's, though, this one gave her no reassurance. "That's one of the men who kidnapped Cora," she told Eli. Eli immediately hit a button his phone, maybe to record the conversation or even try to have it traced.

"That's right," the man said, his voice dripping with sarcasm. "You didn't do what you were supposed to do, so this is about to get very messy."

The muscles in Eli's face went even tighter. "Who are you, and what the hell do you want?"

"Best not to answer either of those on the grounds it might incriminate me." He laughed. "Ready to play, Sergeant Slater?"

"I'd rather know the rules of the game first," Eli fired back.

"Here's the only rule you need to know. Your current houseguest, Ashlyn Darrow, is responsible for this."

She shook her head and was about to insist that she'd done nothing to warrant her child's kidnapping, but then everything inside Ashlyn went still. Eli saw her reaction, too, and he grumbled out more profanity.

"What did Ashlyn do?" Eli demanded.

"That's a question you should ask her," the man said, and with that, he ended the call.

Eli immediately switched back to his brother, and he also aimed her a hard look. "According to Ashlyn, the man who just called me is one of the guys who kidnapped her baby. Can you see the men now?"

"No. But I'm moving in closer. Gunnar's doing the same from the other side. We'll try to pen them in. I'll call you when I can."

The moment Eli ended the call, he gave her another of those looks. "Start explaining."

She shook her head again. "I asked the San Antonio cops for the reports of the night of Marta's murder. And I went to the prison to visit Leon Taggart."

There was no need for her to explain more about that. Leon and Marta were both Eli's criminal informants. Both Marta and Leon had prior drug arrests, but Marta had been small potatoes compared to Leon. And Leon had ultimately been blamed for setting up the ambush attack that'd resulted in the bloodbath the night Marta had been killed.

"Why the hell would you go visit Leon?" Eli asked. She was surprised he could speak with his jaw clenched so tight.

He wasn't going to like her answer.

"I wanted to hear Leon's take on what happened." She paused, because she had to drag in enough breath to continue. "He worked out a plea deal to get the death penalty off the table so there was no trial, no testimony, and I wanted to see if—"

"If I'd been the one to set up what went on that night. You think I purposely had Marta go into that alley so a drug-crazed snake could gun her down."

That thought had kept crossing her mind until she'd become obsessed with it. "I just had to know the truth."

"And you thought you'd get that truth from a criminal with a long record. One who confessed to putting Marta on the scene because he didn't like the competition. She was giving the Rangers and cops more reliable info and therefore getting paid more than he was, and he wanted to put her out of commission."

Ashlyn hadn't expected Eli to see it any other way. But then, he hadn't nearly been killed that night. "I had to be sure." Her gaze flew to his. "And this proves I'm right. There is something off, or why would these men have taken Cora?"

That felt like a punch to the stomach. Oh God. In her quest to find the truth, she'd put her precious baby in danger.

"Why go and visit Leon now?" Eli pressed, not answering her question. "It's been nearly two years."

Ashlyn wasn't sure he would understand. Heck, she wasn't sure she did, either, but enough time had passed that she'd finally felt able to start confronting some of her demons. Cora was responsible for that. Ashlyn hadn't wanted her daughter to be burdened with her mom's emotional baggage, and she'd thought the way to start dealing with that was to visit Leon.

Before Ashlyn could even attempt to answer Eli, she saw him shift his body a little, changing the angle of the view he had outside the window. He had his attention focused on something, or maybe someone, and he was suddenly so still. Holding his breath and waiting.

"Get all the way down to the floor," Eli suddenly shouted. He scrambled toward her.

His loud voice woke Cora, and the baby started to cry again, but Eli's shout wasn't nearly as deafening as the next sound.

A gunshot.

It blasted through the window where he'd just

been standing. A second and third one quickly followed. And the shots set off the security system. The alarms immediately began to blare through the house.

Eli practically threw himself over Cora and her. Good thing, too, because the bullets sent glass flying through the room, and it clattered and pinged to the floor next to her. It no doubt hit Eli, too. She hoped those hits had only come from the glass and not the shots.

As the bullets continued to slam into the house, he turned, pivoting so that his back was to her, and he took aim at the door. It didn't take her long to figure out why he'd done that. The latest shots were hitting the door. It was as if the gunman was trying to tear right through the wood.

And there was something else...

"Is the shooter getting closer?" she asked, her voice trembling. Plus, the alarm was so loud that she wasn't sure how he'd managed to hear her.

"Yeah," he verified.

Oh, mercy. Closer meant he could maybe get into the house and gun them down. Cora could be hurt.

Eli used his phone to turn off the blaring alarms. Probably so he could hear the gunman if he made it onto the porch.

"Move behind the sofa," he instructed. "If things get bad, crawl down the hall and go into my bathroom. Get in the tub."

She nodded and moved as he'd said, but things were already bad. The shots were coming nonstop.

"Where're Kellan and Gunnar?" she asked.

"I'm not sure, but some of those shots are theirs," he explained.

Ashlyn listened. That was hard to do with her pulse crashing in her ears, but she thought she could hear the different firearms. It meant Kellan and the deputy were in a gunfight with these men, but they weren't stopping the one shooting through the door. The one who no doubt had the rifle.

Eli scrambled away from her again, heading back to the window. Putting himself in the line of fire, but a moment later she heard him deliver his own shot. It was even louder than the others had been, and it caused Cora to cry harder. Ashlyn tried to soothe the baby by rocking her, but the noise had obviously frightened her.

When Eli's phone rang, he put the call on speaker, and she braced herself in case it was from the kidnapper. But it was Kellan.

"Hold your fire," Kellan immediately said. "The shooter with the rifle is on the run, and Gunnar and I are moving in. But keep watch. We lost sight of the other one."

"Where'd you last see him?" Eli asked.

Kellan didn't even pause. "He was headed toward your house."

Chapter Three

Eli had figured the danger wasn't over, but he sure as hell hadn't expected one of the thugs to come toward the house when he had two cops in pursuit and another lawman waiting for him inside. The smart thing to do would have been to try to escape, but this guy wasn't doing that. That made him either an idiot, cocky or desperate.

None of those was a good option. All three would be the perfect bad storm, especially considering the guy was armed and ready to commit murder.

Eli fired glances all around the yard. No sign of the man, but Eli knew he was out there somewhere, and if his brother and Gunnar were in pursuit of the other gunman, then that meant Eli needed to make sure this clown didn't get anywhere near Ashlyn and the baby.

He made a quick look over his shoulder at them, to make sure they were still behind the sofa. They were. But now that the security alarms weren't blaring through the house and no one was shooting at them, he could hear Ashlyn's ragged breaths and the baby's whimpers.

Hell.

Ashlyn had to be terrified, perhaps even getting some flashbacks of the night she'd been shot. And that wasn't even the worst of it, because this was a parent's worst nightmare, to have a child in the middle of an attack.

No baby should be put through this, and once he had the situation under control, he needed to make sure it never happened again. That's why he wanted to take the gunman alive. Maybe Kellan and Gunnar could do the same so they could pit the two against each other and get to the truth. Maybe, too, this wouldn't be connected to Marta's murder, but it wasn't looking that way.

Your current houseguest, Ashlyn Darrow, is responsible for this, the kidnapper had said.

Eli didn't intend to just accept the word of a guy trying to kill him, but it left him with an even more unsettled feeling. Had Ashlyn really triggered this by digging into the old case file or visiting Leon? And if so, why would it have caused someone to respond with violence like this?

Leon was in prison. Locked up in a maximum security facility where he was serving a life sentence. It was exactly where he belonged since he'd been the one who'd lured Marta, and therefore Ashlyn and Eli, into that alley with the drug dealer. No way could Leon dispute that, either, because there'd been multiple witnesses.

But Leon had always claimed that he'd been set up.

There'd never been an ounce of proof to that claim and plenty of evidence to indicate Leon had simply wanted Marta dead because he resented her and also because she was about to rat him out for his new criminal association with the drug dealer who'd been killed. Still, it chewed away at Eli that there could be something else about the violence that'd gone on that night. Something he'd missed.

Something that had led to the situation they were in now.

Eli was so focused on watching for the gunman that the sound of the bullet was an unexpected jolt. It caused Ashlyn to gasp.

"The shot wasn't fired near the house," he told her.

It had come from the east side of his land, probably where his brother and Gunnar were. Eli prayed that one of them hadn't been shot. He figured Ashlyn was doing plenty of praying, too, because he heard her mumbling. Also heard her whispering reassurances to the baby.

There was another shot. Also in the distance. But it had no sooner rung out when Eli finally saw something. Not Kellan or Gunnar. This was a man wearing camo who was doing a low military-style crawl on the ground by a line of trees on the side of the house. He was close.

Too close.

Eli shifted and took aim out what had once been a window. It was now just a gaping hole from the other rounds of gunfire. And he waited for a clean shot, maybe to the guy's shoulder. Something to slow him down enough so that Eli could get out there and disarm him.

His phone beeped with a text message, and since Eli didn't want to take his attention off the crawler, he slid his phone across the floor to Ashlyn.

"It's from Kellan," she relayed a moment later. Her breath gusted even more. "He had to kill the shooter."

Eli groaned, but he'd known that could be the likely outcome. That's why it was even more important to keep thug number two alive.

"Kellan and Gunnar are on the way back here," Ashlyn added.

"Text him back and tell him that I've got the gunman in my sight, and he's on the west side of the house in the cluster of pecan trees."

He immediately heard her do that, and Eli knew it would send Kellan and Gunnar that direction. Maybe if the thug knew he had three lawmen bearing down on him, he'd surrender.

Or not.

No sooner had that thought popped into Eli's head, the gunman moved out of the crawling position to crouch behind one of the trees. No doubt getting into position to continue the attack. Continuing it didn't take long, either. It was only a couple of seconds before the guy leaned out and took aim at the house.

Eli couldn't risk another bullet being fired this close to the house, because it could go through the walls and hit the baby. That's why Eli fired first. His shot slammed into the guy's shoulder, just as he'd planned, but the gunman didn't go down. Instead, he lifted his gun again, ready to take the shot that Eli couldn't let him take. Eli tapped his trigger again, sending another bullet into the man's chest.

That put him on the ground.

Cursing, Eli took out Ashlyn's gun, and as he'd done with the phone, he slid it across the floor to her. "Stay put," he warned her, and hoped that she would listen. She probably would only because she wouldn't want to risk taking the baby outside.

"Be careful," she said, but that didn't sound like her first choice of things to tell him. Right now, she likely just wanted him to stay alive so there'd be someone to help her protect the baby.

When she peered out from the sofa to get the gun, he saw the uncertainty in her eyes. Probably because she knew that his going out there was a risk. One he had to take so that he could get to the shooter before the guy bled out. A dead man wouldn't be able to give him any answers.

"Kellan's almost certainly already done it, but go ahead and call for an ambulance," Eli instructed.

Eli heard her do that, too, while he did a quick mental check of the security of the house. The place was all locked up except for the front window with the shattered glass. It wasn't a big enough hole for someone to climb through, but he'd need to keep watch just in case there was a third thug, lying in wait.

That definitely didn't help loosen the knot in his stomach.

Eli unlocked the front door, glanced around. And he listened. There was nothing other than the groans of pain coming from the injured gunman. Those moans let Eli know that the guy was still alive. Probably still armed, too, and that's why Eli couldn't just go charging toward him.

He gave the living room one last glance to make sure Ashlyn was still behind cover. She was and was no longer peering out from the sofa. And with that safeguard ticked off his mental to-do list, he walked out on the porch. His foot brushed against the side of the baby carrier, a reminder that it needed to be processed for trace and fiber evidence, and he took the steps one at a time while still keeping watch.

The gunman groaned again, and as Eli got closer, he saw the guy was lying on his back and clutching his chest. And yeah, he still had a gun in his hand. A gun now soaked in blood. Eli had hoped he'd been wearing a Kevlar vest and had only had the breath knocked out of him. But this was much more serious than that.

The man was dying.

Eli didn't feel any sympathy for the man, this clown who'd come to his house with guns blazing, but he wanted him to hang on.

By the time Eli reached the man, he heard the hurried footsteps behind him. Eli automatically pivoted, his heart jumping to his throat with a fresh slam of adrenaline, but it was just Kellan and Gunnar.

"The ambulance is on the way," Kellan relayed, but then he cursed when he saw the man. And the blood. The guy would be dead before the ambulance could get there.

"Wait on the porch," Eli told Gunnar. "Ashlyn is inside with her baby."

Gunnar nodded and ran to the door to stand guard in what Eli hoped would be an unnecessary precaution. Eli and Kellan continued to the man, and the first thing Eli did was take the gun from his hand because a dying man could still be dangerous and pull a trigger.

Kellan had a small flashlight that he aimed at the shooter's face. Brown hair, nondescript features except for a scar that cut through his right eyebrow. Eli was certain that he'd never seen him before.

"Who are you?" Eli demanded.

The guy managed a sneer. "I got a family," he said. "And you won't get an ID off me from my prints. No record."

Even though it wasn't an answer to his question, that response told Eli plenty. This was a hired gun, and his family would get a payout whether he lived or died. Or at least that's what this clown believed.

"Once you're dead, your face will be plastered on every news station in the state," Eli warned him. "Someone will recognize you, and once I have an ID, I can and will go after your family as accessories to kidnapping and attempted murder of a Texas Ranger. How do you think that'll play out for you, for them, huh?"

No sneer this time, but the guy did cough, and there was a rattling sound in his chest while his hands stayed pressed to his wound. "My family had nothing to do with this. You were just the job."

"Funny, but it felt very personal to me." Eli knelt down, got right in his face and made sure he looked like the badass Ranger that he was. "You endangered an innocent baby. I won't forget that, and I'll go after your family until I put every last one of them in a cage. Now tell me who the hell you are and why you did this."

The man shook his head, dragged in a ragged

breath, but Eli saw the realization in his dying eyes. The realization that Eli wasn't bluffing. "I'm Abe Franklin," he finally said, his voice barely audible now. "And if I tell you who hired me, you have to promise to protect my family. Promise me," he repeated.

Eli would have lied to get the name of the guy's boss, but in this case, no lie was necessary. If his family was indeed innocent, then they'd be protected. "I promise," Eli assured him.

Even though the man clearly only had a few seconds left, he still took his time answering. "The woman with the kid, Ashlyn Darrow, was supposed to shoot and kill you once she thought you'd taken the baby. And then the woman would be arrested for your murder."

Eli had already come up with that theory, but it didn't give him the info he needed. "Who set that up? Who hired you?"

"She said you and Ashlyn wouldn't see it coming, that you wouldn't suspect her at all."

"She?" Eli demanded.

"The woman who hired me. She said you wouldn't suspect her because you thought she was dead." The next breath was much thinner. The cough, more of a death rattle. "Her name is Marta Seaver."

Chapter Four

Ashlyn eased Cora into the infant seat that Eli had arranged to have in the back seat of the cruiser. The baby remained asleep, thank goodness, and Ashlyn hoped she stayed that way for the next couple of hours. Cora had already had enough interruptions to her routine and sleep.

Even though it would only be a short drive from the hospital where they'd just been examined to the sheriff's office, Eli had insisted on them riding in the bullet-resistant cruiser. He'd told Ashlyn that he didn't want to take any chances. Since her baby's life could be at risk, neither did she.

But Ashlyn wanted to know why there was that dangerous risk in the first place.

And who was really behind it.

She hated that the hired thug claimed that Marta was his boss. Hated even more the man had died before giving them the truth. Of course, to him maybe that was the truth. The person who hired him could have told him that. It was just as possible, though, that he'd used his dying breath to lie.

Judging from the phone calls Eli was making, he was considering that it was at least a possibility that Marta was alive.

On the drive to the hospital and during Cora's exam in the ER, Eli hadn't left their sides. He'd stood guard, continuing to keep watch. That gave Ashlyn the chance to hear him contact the admin office at the San Antonio hospital where Marta had been pronounced dead. When he hadn't been able to reach someone who had answers, he'd left messages both there and then at the funeral home that had handled Marta's remains.

She listened to those calls and others he made. Some to the two CSI teams who were at her house and his to remind them to relay to him anything that they found. He'd done the same to the medical examiner and his brother Kellan. Ashlyn had no doubts that he would get that info.

However, what concerned her was that it wouldn't keep her daughter out of further danger.

When her mouth began to tremble and the tears threatened, again, Ashlyn clamped her teeth over her bottom lip and forced herself to stay steady. It wouldn't help anything if she fell apart, and it would likely only rile Eli even more. He was obviously upset, not just at the attack but probably at her, too.

She'd been a fool to believe those thugs when they'd told her Eli had kidnapped Cora.

And it could have gotten Eli killed.

Ashlyn hated to think that she would have pulled the trigger, but she'd been out of her mind with fear and worry when she'd driven to his house. If Eli and she had gotten into a scuffle... But she stopped herself from going there. It hadn't happened, period, and she didn't need to play "what if."

"Marta's dead," Ashlyn repeated once Eli had finished his latest call to the crime lab.

Eli made a sound of agreement. It was the same reaction he'd had the first time she pointed out that obvious fact shortly after he had told her what the gunman said. Eli definitely hadn't argued with her then, or now.

"But you called the funeral home and the San Antonio hospital," she pointed out. "So you must think her being alive is at least a possibility."

He made another of those annoying noncommittal sounds but then glanced at her. Well, actually his glance went to Cora first, then her. "Just covering all the bases." He paused and didn't say anything else until his attention was back at keeping watch out the window. "I checked Marta's pulse that night and didn't feel one."

Ashlyn had known he'd done that. Once backup had arrived, Eli had stooped down and touched his fingers to Marta's neck. He hadn't said anything, but Ashlyn had seen it in his eyes. The dread. The grief.

The guilt.

Or maybe she'd seen the guilt only because she had blamed him for what had happened to Marta. Ashlyn still did blame him. Though it was hard to hang on to every drop of that blame after what Eli had done tonight. He'd put his life on the line for Cora and her.

"Thank you for protecting Cora," she said.

The next sound he made seemed to be one of dismissal. It had an "I was just doing my job" ring to it, and maybe that's all it was, but at the core of it was something very personal. A different kind of personal than the old attractions that had once been between them.

She and Eli had been in that alley when Marta was shot. When she'd been shot, too. And whether either of them wanted it, it had created this connection between them. One that came with bad memories and a shared nightmare that was still haunting them. Maybe it always would.

While Gunnar drove down Main Street, Eli continued to keep watch, and he checked his phone whenever it dinged with a text message. Since Cora's car seat was between them, Ashlyn couldn't see what was on his phone screen, but she could certainly see Eli. The muscles flexing in his jaw. The tightness of his mouth. The formidable expression.

She'd always thought he had the face of a warrior, and that was especially true now. Like all his brothers, he had the cocoa-brown hair and stormy gray eyes, but there was an edge to Eli. Something unsettled. He was dangerous-looking. As if the only thing he was searching for was the next fight. A fight he was certain he would win.

Maybe it was the adrenaline and fatigue, but Ashlyn remembered when he'd kissed her. So many years ago. They'd been practically kids, and it was something that the bad memories of Marta should have washed away.

But it hadn't.

He'd kissed like a warrior, too.

"Are you okay?" Gunnar asked.

It took Ashlyn a couple of seconds to realize he was talking to her and that he was volleying glances at her in the rearview mirror. Heaven knew what her expression must have been for him to ask that now, but she hoped she hadn't shown any signs of remembering that warrior kiss from Eli.

"I'm just tired," she settled for saying.

Gunnar nodded. "Once Kellan gets your statement, maybe we can find a place for you to take a nap."

She doubted she'd be able to sleep, but Gunnar's comment told her that she probably wouldn't be leaving the sheriff's office before morning. Not that she especially wanted to leave. Ashlyn definitely didn't want to go back to her house until they'd figured out why this attack had happened.

Or if there'd be another one.

"Remy will be coming in for questioning," Eli told her after he read another text on his phone.

Ashlyn immediately shook her head and tried to process that. Eli didn't have to explain who Remy was. She knew. Remy Sager was Marta's boyfriend, and he'd been crushed when she died. And in a rage from the pain of losing the woman he loved.

"You actually think Remy had something to do with the attack?" Ashlyn asked.

"Just covering all the bases," Eli repeated.

She supposed he had to start the investigation somewhere, and with both gunmen dead, Eli would need to find the reason for the attack. But Remy seemed as much of a long shot as contacting the funeral home and the San Antonio hospital.

"Has Remy threatened you recently?" she asked.

Eli shook his head. "But it's hard to know what's in a person's mind. Some people don't just jump right into revenge. They stew on it for a while and then come at you when you're not expecting it."

Maybe, but it didn't make sense in this case. "Remy didn't hold a grudge against me, and he never threatened me. Whoever did this wanted me to kill you. You would have been dead, and I would have gone to jail. The grudge or whatever this is seems to be against both of us."

A grudge that was a sick kind of poetic justice to have her end up killing the man that she had blamed for Marta's death. Well, in part she had blamed him, anyway, but Remy had put the full blame on Eli. Ashlyn hadn't witnessed firsthand the exchanges between Eli and him because she'd been in the hospital recovering, but some of the nurses had told her about Remy's accusations and threats against Eli. Then the cops from San Antonio PD had brought it up, too, when they'd interviewed her.

"Remy could have let his grief fester to the point that he wants someone else to pay for Marta's death," Eli pointed out. His voice was calm enough, but she figured that was a facade. Someone had just tried to kill them, and that had to eat away at him. Plus, he would want to get the bottom of it, and that meant taking a hard look at Remy. Doing so would dredge up the past and put the nightmarish memories right in front of them again.

Gunnar pulled to a stop in front of the sheriff's office, and as Eli had done at his house and at the hospital, he positioned himself in front of her when she scooped the baby into her arms. He kept right by Cora and her when they hurried inside, where she immediately spotted Kellan in the doorway of his office.

The bullpen was empty, which likely meant everyone other than Gunnar and Kellan was out working the investigation. No sign of Eli's other brother,

Owen, who was a deputy, and she hoped he was home with his toddler daughter. Since Owen lived just a short distance from Eli, Ashlyn wanted him to stay close to home in case something else went wrong. Whoever was carrying out this grudge—or whatever it was—might use Owen to get to them.

Kellan didn't waste any time, and he quickly ushered them into his office. Away from the front door and the windows. A reminder that another gunman could be out there. That didn't help calm any of her still-raw nerves.

"The doctor said Ashlyn and the baby weren't hurt," Eli relayed to his brother the moment Kellan shut his office door behind him.

Kellan nodded and motioned for Ashlyn to take the chair across from his desk. Because her legs felt as if they might give way, she did. "I'll need diapers and a bottle for her soon," she let them know.

Kellan gave another nod. "What kind of formula and diapers?"

After Ashlyn told him, he fired off a message to someone, most likely arranging for those items, and then he turned to Eli. "Remy won't be in until nine in the morning," Kellan explained. "And he's bringing his lawyer with him."

That didn't surprise her. Word of the attack had almost certainly gotten out, and Remy would know that he would be a suspect.

"If Remy did this, he'll have an alibi," Ashlyn

said, and judging from the quick looks of approval, Eli and Kellan had already considered that.

"We'll get his financials," Eli assured her. "If Remy paid for those thugs, we'll find it."

She didn't have any idea how much it cost to hire would-be killers, but Ashlyn suspected it would be enough of a withdrawal to get their attention. That meant Remy would have covered those tracks, too. Except there was a problem with the whole theory that Remy was responsible for this.

"Remy isn't rich," she reminded them, her gaze holding on Eli. "From what I've heard, he drained his savings trying to bring a civil lawsuit against you." A lawsuit for Marta's wrongful death that a judge had dismissed before it could even go to trial.

If Eli had a reaction to the reminder of the legal attempt against him, he didn't show it. He kept the same stony expression he'd had in the cruiser. "He could have borrowed the money or sold something to get it," Eli pointed out just as quickly. He turned to his brother. "SAPD is interviewing Abe Franklin's family. They might know who actually hired him."

Ashlyn latched onto that hope even though she knew it was a long shot. "What about the second gunman?"

Kellan glanced at his computer screen, his eyes scanning over the info he saw there. "Charles Cardona. He's got a record as long as Abe Franklin's.

No family other than an ex-wife. The Austin PD will interview her."

So, the investigation was already in full swing. No surprise there, since someone had targeted a Texas Ranger. Law enforcement all over the state would hopefully see this attack on one of their own, and that would spur them to get to the bottom of it ASAP.

Eli and Kellan exchanged a glance, and it seemed as if something passed between them. A cue, maybe, because Eli turned to her. "Tell us about the baby," Eli insisted.

Ashlyn felt herself go stiff, and she tightened her grip around Cora. His comment definitely didn't sound friendly, more like a lawman's order. "I adopted her six weeks ago. She's three months old."

They both stared at her, definitely waiting for more, and the uneasy feeling in her stomach turned to a hard knot. Because she suddenly knew why they had those lawmen eyes on her.

"Dominick McComb," she muttered. Just saying his name tightened her stomach even more, but Ashlyn shook her head. "He's Cora's biological grandfather, and he wasn't happy about the adoption. But he wouldn't have done this. He wouldn't have done anything to put Cora at risk."

Eli lifted his shoulder as if maybe not buying that. "Why wasn't he happy about the adoption?"

Obviously, they weren't going to accept that

Dominick was innocent. And maybe Ashlyn didn't, either, but it chilled her breath to bone to even consider that Dominick might be behind this. Unlike Remy, Dominick had money along with a cool facade that didn't make cops take a second look at him. That made him even more dangerous than Remy, but she didn't think that danger would apply to anything he did with Cora.

Ashlyn took a moment to steady herself before she answered. "Cora's biological parents were Olive Landry and Dominick's son, Danny. Danny died of a drug overdose when Olive was pregnant, so Olive decided she'd put the baby up for adoption. Olive and I met, and she liked me. She's a college student, only nineteen," Ashlyn added.

"Olive didn't want Dominick to raise the child?" Eli pressed.

"No, and neither did Danny," Ashlyn said without hesitation. "Dominick has a police record, and Olive thought he, well, bullied Danny. Dominick tried to stop the adoption, but that didn't go anywhere."

"A judge denied him custody," Eli spelled out. "But he does have supervised visitations." Obviously, he'd gotten that information during one of those many calls he'd made.

Ashlyn nodded. "He sees Cora every two weeks. But not alone. When he visits, I'm there, and so is a social worker. And then there's the nanny he hired."

"A nanny?" Eli questioned. Obviously, that wasn't something Eli had known, and he was probably wondering why a man with very limited, supervised visits would need the services of a nanny.

"His visits weren't long, only an hour each time, but Dominick was hoping that Cora would eventually have overnight stays at his house. He thought it was a good idea to have a nanny in place, one who already knew Cora." She paused. "He's never been hostile toward me. And he's very loving with Cora. That's why I don't believe Dominick would have hired those men."

"Maybe the gunmen didn't have orders to fire into the house or endanger the baby." Eli's argument came so fast that she realized he'd already given this some thought. "Unlike Remy, Dominick has the funds to hire thugs."

Yes, he did, and she couldn't completely dismiss the notion that the thugs hadn't followed orders. Maybe they panicked when things hadn't gone as planned. Still...

"Why would Dominick have sent gunmen after you?" she asked Eli. "He doesn't even know you."

"Dominick doesn't have to know me, but I'm sure he's heard of me," Eli assured her.

He let that hang in the air, and Ashlyn tried to figure out his train of thought. It didn't take her long to do that. It'd been all over the news about Marta's death, and Dominick could have easily found out the details with some simple internet searches. If Ashlyn had indeed murdered Eli, she would be in jail. Maybe even dead. The gunmen could have been instructed to kill her and make it look like a suicide because she was so distraught over killing Eli.

And then she would have no longer been in the way of a custody challenge from Dominick.

His police record and Olive's wishes might be dismissed with the adoptive mother out of the way. Dominick could even possibly use this as a way of discrediting Olive and accusing her of handing over Cora to someone mentally unstable enough to commit murder.

"Oh God," Ashlyn said under her breath.

"Yeah," Eli agreed. Obviously, he'd had no trouble figuring out what was going through her head. "He'll be brought in for questioning, too. And since Dominick does have the money to hire more guns, Cora and you will need to be in protective custody. For the time being, that'll be with me."

Her head snapped up, and she fired a glance first at Eli, then Kellan. "Eli insisted," Kellan explained.

"I'm seeing this through to the end," Eli added when her attention shifted back to him. "No one puts a baby in danger and then tries to kill me. Whoever's behind this won't get away with it."

She wasn't sure if that was a threat or a promise. Maybe it was both. But before Ashlyn could point out the problems of the two of them being under the same roof, there was a knock on the door. The sound caused her to gasp, a reminder of just how on edge she still was. Her body tensed, bracing for a fight, but it wasn't a threat. It was Gunnar.

"Here are the baby supplies," Gunnar said, holding up several large bags. "Want me to put them in the cruiser?"

Eli nodded. "You'll be driving us to Jack's?"

"Jack?" Ashlyn repeated. She knew who he was, of course. Marshal Jack Slater, another of Eli's brothers, and he lived on the grounds of their family ranch.

"We're going to his place," Eli verified. "He's out of town on a case, and he said we could use it. We can't go back to our houses because the CSIs are still there."

She didn't want to go to their houses, but she was still shaking her head about Jack's. "What if hired guns follow us there?"

"We'll take precautions." Eli's gaze held for several moments on Cora. "Lots of them. Trust me, keeping your daughter safe is my top priority."

Ashlyn heard the unspoken part of that. He wanted her to put aside their pasts and declare a truce. For Cora. That was probably the only thing that could have caused her to nod.

"Thank you," she managed to tell Eli.

Obviously, he wasn't comfortable with that because his mouth tightened again. "Are you okay with Ashlyn giving her statement tomorrow?" Eli asked Kellan, and he checked the time. "It's late, and I'm sure we could all use some rest."

"Tomorrow's fine," Kellan agreed, and he looked up at Gunnar. "Stay there with them tonight at Jack's. I'll get someone out there to relieve you first thing in the morning."

Ashlyn stood to get ready to leave, but she stopped when Eli's phone dinged with a text message. He frowned, then scowled when he read it and then immediately made a call. She hadn't been able to see what was on his phone screen, but Ashlyn held her breath, praying this wasn't the start of another attack.

"What the hell do you mean by a glitch?" Eli snapped to the person that he'd called.

The next part of the conversation was all one-sided so Ashlyn looked at Kellan to see if he knew what was going on. He shook his head, lifted his shoulder.

"Find them now," Eli growled a couple of seconds later, and he stabbed the End Call button as if he'd declared war on it. There was an angry fire in stormy eyes.

"What's wrong?" Kellan and she asked in unison.

A tight muscle flickered in Eli's jaw. "Marta's funeral home and hospital records are missing. Both the hard copies and the digital files. It looks as if someone stole them."

Chapter Five

Eli's fun meter was already at zero, and hearing about Marta's missing files sure as hell didn't give his mood a boost. He wanted answers, damn it, and this certainly wasn't helping.

Neither were his sleeping arrangements for the night.

Of course, Eli seriously doubted that he'd be getting much sleep, but he was going to need at least a nap if he wanted his brain to continue to function. And that nap would need to happen at his brother's house. With Ashlyn and her baby daughter under the same roof.

Ashlyn didn't look any more pleased than he did about the sleeping arrangements when Eli ushered her into the wood-and-stone house, and Eli knew her disapproval wasn't because of the place itself. She was no doubt troubled by that "being under the same roof" part, too.

He stepped in, glanced around, trying to see it

from a lawman's eyes rather than a visitor's. It definitely wasn't sprawling like the main house where Kellan lived and helped run the family ranch. This one only had a combined living and kitchen area, two bedrooms, an office, two baths and was, well, laid-back. Which was a fairly apt description of his brother Jack. This was a place where you could flop on the sofa, drink a beer and watch the game on the big-screen TV mounted on the wall above the fireplace.

Now it was going to be a place where Eli would keep Ashlyn and Cora safe. He started that by arming the security system, which he knew was top-notch. It was a precaution that Eli and all his brothers had taken after their father was murdered.

"I'll put these in the guest room," Gunnar said, holding up the bags of baby supplies. "I'll also close the curtains and make sure all the doors and windows are locked," the deputy added, and he went into the hall.

"You really believe Marta's missing records are a glitch?" Ashlyn came and asked Eli. It was just a rephrasing of what she'd already pressed him on, and during one of his responses, Eli had indeed used the word *glitch*.

His word choice, though, was because the alternative just pissed him off. There was no good reason for someone to steal the files. That's why he'd demanded a full investigation on it. However, there was a bad reason for a person to do this.

"I don't believe Marta's alive," he said. "But someone could have stolen and wiped the files to muddy the waters." If he had to run down leads on who'd do something like that, then he wasn't focusing on the actual person who'd sent those armed idiots after them.

She nodded, swallowed hard and then glanced around as if to give herself a distraction. "The place looks like Jack."

It didn't surprise him that she would realize that since she knew his brothers as well as she did him. Almost as well, he mentally corrected, since she hadn't been around them much lately. However, Ashlyn had been Eli's girlfriend in high school.

Now he mentally cursed.

Because he had to add an asterisk to that girlfriend label. She'd lost her virginity to him when she was seventeen, a memory that was certainly etched in his brain. His body wasn't going to let him forget it, either.

Once, they'd been as close as a couple could be, and while Eli hadn't exactly been planning their future when he'd been in high school, it had stung when they'd drifted apart after Ashlyn had gone off to college. Then there'd been other relationships, both his and hers, and the timing hadn't worked for them to get together for even a round of ex-sex.

Then Marta had died, and everything had gone to hell in a handbasket.

He'd never been thankful for the bad blood between them, but it would stop the old heat from rising now. He hoped. Because that wasn't a distraction he needed when he already had enough of them.

"Will we really be okay here?" she asked, and even though he'd purposely kept the light dim, he had no trouble seeing the fear that was still in her eyes. "I want the truth. Don't tell me something just to ease my mind."

He thought about that a moment, then nodded. "No mind-easing then. The security system will alert us if anyone tries to break in. Both Gunnar and I will be here, and we'll both have our guns ready."

Their gazes met. Held. "Will that be enough?" she asked. Ashlyn pulled the baby even closer to her. "Because nothing bad can happen to Cora. I can't lose her."

The fear was in her voice, too. And the love. Eli recognized it because his brother Owen had a daughter as well, and he got an up close and personal look at that parental love whenever he visited them.

"It'll be enough," Eli assured her. It wasn't a lie. He hoped. And because he didn't want her to see any doubts in him, he tipped his head to the hall. "As soon as Gunnar's done checking the place, I'll show you to the guest room. You'll feel better once you've gotten some rest."

She nodded, almost absently, and with the baby cuddled in her arms, she went to the bookshelves on the sides of the fireplace. Her gaze combed over the framed pictures, some of Eli and his brothers. Others were of the champion horses that Jack had raised and trained.

Her attention lingered on the one that was on the center shelf. It was a shot of Kellan and his now fiancée, Gemma, and they were standing next to Jack and his then-lover, Caroline Moser. It had obviously been taken during happier times, because they were all smiling.

"Caroline Moser," Ashlyn said. She looked at him. "How is Jack?"

Eli knew that was a Texas-sized question with a couple of layers. Their father had been murdered a little over a year ago, and his killer still hadn't been caught. Ironic, since Eli and all his brothers were lawmen.

"Jack's okay," Eli answered, but he had no idea if that was even true. That's because the one person who could tell them their father's killer was Caroline, and a head injury prevented her from remembering.

Ashlyn's glance was more of a flat look to let him know that she didn't buy the part about Jack being okay. Or any of them, for that matter. They'd lost their father and couldn't bring his killer to justice. That ate away at all of them. Eli liked to think that he had less in the eating away department because he was still feeling lower than dirt about Marta's murder. Both deaths, though, had left plenty of holes in him.

"It's all clear," Gunnar announced when he came back into the living room. He tipped his head to the sofa. "I'll crash in here for a while. That way, I can hear if anyone drives up."

Eli had been about to make the same offer, but since Gunnar got to it first, he'd crash on the floor outside where Ashlyn would be. Jack wouldn't mind if Eli slept in his bed, but the master was at the end of the hall with the office in between it and the guest room. Until Eli was certain there was no longer a threat, he didn't want to be that far away from Ashlyn and Cora.

He led Ashlyn into the guest room and immediately saw a problem. "Sorry, no crib. I can try to get one—"

"No. It's okay. We won't be here that long."

It sounded as if she had some other plan in mind. Or maybe it was just wishful thinking. Either way, he didn't press it.

"I can put Cora on a quilt on the floor," Ashlyn added, and she brushed a kiss on the baby's head. "I don't want her on the bed because she's started to roll over, and she might fall off."

Since she had her hands full, Eli helped with the bedding issue. There was an extra cover folded on top of the dresser, and he spread it out on the floor. He was pretty sure he'd find some more bedding in the hall closet for Gunnar and him.

"The bathroom's attached," Eli explained, tipping his head to one of the doors. "Don't know if it's got what you need, but if not, let me know and I'll have one of the ranch hands bring it over."

Ashlyn nodded again and muttered a thanks. "What happens next?" she asked just as Eli had turned to leave. "About the investigation," she clarified when he stared at her.

Hell. For just a split second, he'd let the old heat creep into his body, and it was a reminder of how easy it would be to lose focus.

"I'll see if Kellan has any updates. Then I need to make some calls to the hospital and funeral home. I want to talk personally to the folks who dealt with Marta's records." And he didn't give a rat that it was the wee hours of the morning. He wanted answers right away.

"You'll let me know if you find anything?" she pressed.

He nodded and got out of there. The best way to regain focus was to put some distance between Ashlyn and him. Of course, there was no chance his body was going to let him forget that she was just a door away.

Eli went back into the living area where Gunnar was already stretched out on the sofa. Not asleep yet, but from the looks of it, he soon would be, so Eli went into the laundry room just off the kitchen to make his calls. He tried the contact number at the hospital first.

No answer. Which didn't please him.

That displeasure went up a significant notch when the answering service for the funeral home transferred his call, only to have it unanswered as well. It went to voice mail, and Eli left a scathing message for the person in charge to call him immediately. If he hadn't heard from them in a few hours, he would have SAPD go to the place with a search warrant. A warrant he was certain that he could get since he could tie it to the attack tonight.

Eli was about to try Kellan next, but before he could do that, his phone buzzed, and he saw his brother's name on the screen. Good. Well, maybe. He hoped Kellan wasn't calling with more bad news.

"It looks like we got a break," Kellan said the moment that Eli answered. "I'm sending you something that I'm sure you'll want to see."

WHEN CORA GRINNED at her and flailed her arms and legs in excitement, Ashlyn couldn't help but smile back. She was still shaken from the attack the night before, still trying to get past the fatigue of too little sleep, but it was impossible to stay gloomy when looking at her little girl.

Ashlyn finished dressing the baby, picking her up from the quilt on the floor and giving her kisses on her cheeks and neck. The sound that Cora made wasn't quite a laugh, more of a breathy babble. Like the grin, it also lifted Ashlyn's spirits. Yes, there was a lot of danger and uncertainty right now, but she didn't have a single doubt about the love she felt for her baby.

A child she'd thought she would never have.

It didn't matter that she hadn't been the one to give birth to Cora. The little girl was hers in every way that counted, and she would make sure she was not only safe but happy.

"It's me," Eli said a split second before there was a knock on the door.

"Come in," Ashlyn answered.

He did, almost hesitantly, and he seemed relieved that she was up and dressed. Ashlyn had made sure of that. She'd gotten up before Cora so she could grab a quick shower so that she would be ready to go if something went wrong. And so that Eli wouldn't walk in on her when she was wearing only a T-shirt that she'd slept in.

With his hands crammed in the pockets of his jeans, Eli walked in. Not too close, though. He stood there eyeing Cora while the baby eyed him. Ashlyn studied him as well and wished that she hadn't.

Mercy, no one should look that good after the horrible night they'd had. Yet he managed it in his jeans that were snug and loose in all the right places. The gray shirt also had a too-good fit, and it was nearly the same color as his eyes. The top three buttons were undone, but in her mind it was as if it were fully open so she could see his chest—which she knew was as incredible as the rest of him.

He followed her gaze, nearly causing her to curse because he'd caught her gawking at him, but then Eli only shrugged. "I raided Jack's closet for some clean clothes."

Oh, so maybe he hadn't realized the gawking after all. Good. There was enough heat still stirring between them without her adding that to the mix.

Cora made another of those cooing babbles and reached out a hand to Eli. Apparently, Cora had the knack for making Eli smile, too, because the corner of his mouth hitched, and he went to them, sinking down onto the floor. He stunned Ashlyn when he pulled Cora into his arms.

"She's a cute kid," Eli muttered. "And she smells good."

It took Ashlyn a few seconds to get her mouth working. "Baby soap. There was some in the supplies that Gunnar brought in. I bathed Cora in the bathroom sink." She paused. "You seem pretty comfortable holding a baby."

He shrugged again. "I've had some practice with

Owen's daughter, Addie. She's a year and a half old now, and we've all taken our turns babysitting."

A surprise that Eli would involve himself in that, but then Owen's wife had died in childbirth so he'd likely needed the help.

"Don't puke on me," Eli playfully told Cora as he lifted her into the air.

Cora didn't puke, but she did act as if Eli was the greatest thing since baby formula. The playfulness didn't seem right, not with everything else going on. Not with the old wounds that were still between Eli and her.

Not with the heat.

All the memories began to swirl together, and that's when Ashlyn knew she had to get this back on track. "Any updates on the investigation?" she asked.

"A few. One big one," he added a moment later. He looked at her. "Remy recently came into a lot of money, nearly a hundred grand. It's an inheritance from his grandmother."

She took a moment to process it. That was certainly plenty enough to hire those two gunmen. "When did Remy get this money?"

"A week ago, but he's known it would be coming for several months now."

So he'd had plenty of planning time. Even though she wasn't a cop, Ashlyn had no trouble figuring out that Remy had means, motive and even the opportunity for the kidnapping and attack. Since Marta had been a criminal informant, Remy could have even used Marta's old contacts to find the gunmen.

But Ashlyn immediately rethought that last part.

"Marta didn't associate with violent people," Ashlyn pointed out. "Yes, she'd had an arrest for drug possession when she was eighteen, but she'd turned her life around. She helped the cops. She helped *you*."

"She did," Eli readily admitted, but then he didn't say anything else for several seconds. "But drugs and violence overlap. She knew Leon, who in turn knew Drake Zeller."

Eli didn't spell out for her that Drake had certainly been violent, since he'd been the one who'd shot both Marta and her. Even though Leon hadn't fired any shots, he'd been convicted of setting up the ambush.

"Of course, Leon claims he didn't personally know Drake," Ashlyn reminded him under her breath.

Eli went silent again, and he handed Cora back to her before he stood. Ashlyn expected him to just walk out and put up that wall between them again. But he didn't leave. He put his hands on his hips and glanced up at the ceiling before his attention came back to her.

"I've gone over every detail a thousand times

of that night Marta was killed," he said. "I'm sure you have, too."

She had, and Ashlyn confirmed it with a nod.

"I didn't set up the ambush," Eli went on. "Neither did you or Marta. That leaves Leon, since Drake couldn't have put it together on his own. The anonymous tip I got about the drug bust came through official channels, through a number that only the criminal informants used."

A number that Eli knew—that's what she was about to point out. It was the old argument that Ashlyn had used because she hadn't believed Leon was gutsy enough to do something like that. It was too dangerous, and from everything she'd learned and heard about Leon, he was basically a coward.

But Marta hadn't been.

And now for the first time Ashlyn had to consider this from a different angle. She had to consider the unthinkable. What if Marta had set up the ambush in the alley? And maybe Marta had done that to kill Eli. Of course, Ashlyn couldn't think of a good reason why Marta would want Eli dead, but it was something she needed to at least admit was possible. Along with admitting something else.

What if Marta was still alive?

"Did you find out anything about Marta's missing records?" she asked.

Eli stared at her as if he wasn't pleased with the shift in conversation. Maybe because he'd wanted or hoped for an air-clearing between them. Of course, he probably already knew that the "air" wasn't as murky between them as it had been before the attack. He'd saved her and Cora's lives, and that changed things. So did this old attraction rearing its head. Someday, soon, they'd talk that all out, but for now the investigation had to come first.

He dragged in a long breath before he finally answered. "Terrell Wilburn, the mortician who handled Marta's remains, is on vacation, but I'm in the process of tracking him down so I can question him. The owner doesn't understand why the file is missing, but he said Wilburn might have copies of it. They're looking into it. So am I."

That wasn't a surprise. Eli would dig until he found answers. "And the hospital?" Ashlyn pressed.

"They're sticking with the glitch theory. They're converting from hard copy to digital and think it got lost in the shuffle. I don't believe it."

"You think Marta's alive and there was a cover-up?" she pressed.

"No. But someone might want me to think that. I'm having SAPD show Remy's photo to the employees at both places. Something might pop."

Yes, but it was just as likely that Remy would have hired someone to steal those files. If he was the person behind the attack, that is.

"The cops questioned the families of the two dead gunmen," Eli went on a moment later. "If they know anything about who hired the men, they're hiding it well. If there is something to hide, the Rangers will be monitoring their bank accounts to make sure there aren't any unusual deposits."

Good. Because then a deposit like that could be traced back to the source. Hopefully, anyway.

Eli continued to stare at her as if there was something else he wanted to say. "There's coffee in the kitchen if you want a cup."

She doubted that was what was actually on his mind, but before Ashlyn could press it, his phone dinged with a text message. Whatever he saw on the screen caused his forehead to bunch up.

"Dominick just came into the sheriff's office," Eli relayed. "He's demanding to see you and the baby."

Chapter Six

Eli was absolutely certain he wouldn't like anything about this visit to the sheriff's office. For starters, it put Ashlyn and the baby out of the house and on the road—since she had insisted on making the trip with him.

It was too big a risk.

Of course, so was staying put, as Ashlyn had argued. Getting answers was what they needed if they were to figure out what was going on, but Eli wasn't convinced it was necessary for Ashlyn to go with him to get those answers. Hell, he wasn't sure they'd be getting any useful information from Dominick.

The only thing that was certain so far was that Eli despised the man for demanding to see Ashlyn and the baby. Even more, he hated the new round of worry and fear that this had put in Ashlyn's eyes.

Eli cursed himself when that thought sank in. Now he was thinking about worry, fear and her eyes. None of that would help this investigation.

At least Ashlyn had agreed with him about Dominick not seeing the baby. Actually, she'd been as adamant about that as Eli had been. Until they were certain that Dominick had had no part in hiring those thugs, then he wouldn't have access to his granddaughter.

Eli was betting that wouldn't go over well with Dominick.

And that was the reason he'd taken precautions before they'd left Jack's house. First, he'd called a sitter, Gloria Coyle. The woman hadn't actually watched Cora yet, but Gloria was someone they had both known most of their lives. Ashlyn had contacted her shortly before the adoption to ask her if she'd be able to watch the child if ever there was some kind of emergency. This definitely fell into that "emergency" category, so Gloria had agreed to meet them at the sheriff's office. She could wait with Cora in the break room while Ashlyn chatted with Dominick.

That wouldn't be a fun conversation, either.

After Dominick said whatever it was he had to say to Ashlyn, then Eli wanted a crack at questioning the man. As a Texas Ranger, he didn't have a set jurisdiction, so it would be perfectly legal for him to do that as long as Kellan agreed. Which he would. His brother was as eager to get to the bottom of this as he was.

This time when they arrived at the sheriff's office, Eli had Gunnar park the cruiser at the back of the building. One of the other security measures Eli had taken was to ask Kellan to unlock the back door so he could get Ashlyn and Cora in fast. Kellan had also posted a deputy there to make sure a hired gun hadn't thought it was a good place to lie in wait for an ambush.

When Gunnar pulled to a stop, Eli glanced around for any signs of a threat. None. But he saw his other brother Owen waiting in the doorway. So this was the deputy that Kellan had assigned to the protection detail. Owen immediately stepped out, helping Ashlyn get the baby into the break room. The transfer was fast, exactly what Eli wanted.

Gloria was already there, waiting, and she went to Ashlyn to give her a hug as soon as Owen had shut and locked the door. Ashlyn thanked the woman, and while they talked about the baby's bottle and such, Eli turned to Owen.

"Dominick's in the interview room," Owen said. "He's got a bad attitude and two lawyers." He glanced at the baby. "Please tell me he won't get near that little girl."

"Trust me, he won't," Eli assured him.

There must have been something in his tone that got Owen's attention, because he lifted an eyebrow. "That sounded…personal."

Eli scowled. "Don't read anything into it."

Owen's eyebrow stayed up. "Hey, this is your brother, remember? I used to have to cover for you when you sneaked off with Ashlyn for some…private time."

"That was high school," Eli snapped.

And if they'd been in high school now, that remark from Owen would have earned him a butt-whipping. Not because it wasn't true. It was. But Eli didn't like that smug look on Owen's face. Still, he supposed it was better than the angry gloom and doom that all of them had been sporting since this whole ordeal had begun.

Ashlyn handed off the baby to Gloria, but Eli didn't have to be a mind reader to know that was hard for Ashlyn to do. With the memories still fresh from the attack, she probably didn't want the baby out of her sight. Something he considered using to try to talk her out of coming here to see Dominick, but her expression was easy to read, too, when she looked at him.

She was ready to do this.

"I'll wait back here with Gloria and the baby," Owen assured Ashlyn. "We'll keep the door locked and the security alarm on."

Ashlyn thanked him, and as if it were the most natural thing in the world, she brushed a kiss on Owen's cheek. A reminder that once Ashlyn and his brother had been friends. Heck, maybe they still were. Ashlyn had shut Eli out of her life, but it was possible she hadn't done the same to the rest of his family.

She gave the baby one last kiss and then one last glance before she followed Eli out of the break room. He shut that door, too, so that Dominick wouldn't be able to hear the baby if she cried or fussed.

"Is the adoption ironclad?" Eli asked her as they walked up the hall.

"Yes." She didn't hesitate, but she did give him a long look. "Why do you ask?"

"I just don't want Dominick to spring any surprises on you. I don't want him trying to get temporary custody because he could convince a judge that you can't keep Cora safe."

He expected for that to put some alarm in those already emotion-heavy eyes. It didn't. Ashlyn shook her head. "He has no legal claim."

"What if you were out of the picture?" he added.

Now there was some alarm. "You mean if I were dead." The breath that she blew out was part huff. "It still wouldn't happen." But she didn't sound exactly convinced of that.

Eli wasn't convinced of it, either, and even though Dominick might not have a legal claim to the child, the truth was, the birth mother also wouldn't have a claim, because she'd signed the papers and was the only surviving birth parent. Custody would be up in the air since Ashlyn didn't have any close family heirs. That could create the right amount of custody chaos for Dominick to make his move.

He didn't spell that out for Ashlyn. Planting that

seed was enough to make her even more aware—and skeptical—of anything Dominick said.

When they made it to the interview room, Kellan was already there waiting for them. "Dominick wants to talk to you first," he told Ashlyn, "and then you'll have to leave for the actual interview. You can watch from the observation room though if you like."

She nodded, murmured a thanks, and she walked in behind Kellan when he opened the door. Eli had no trouble spotting Dominick because he recognized him from his driver's license photo that Eli had pulled up during his background search on the man. Dominick was tall with a well-toned build. Despite the thread of gray in his dark brown hair, he looked ten years younger than he actually was.

There were two guys wearing suits on either side of Dominick, and one of them stood when Dominick did. The lawyers gave Eli the once-over with some stink eye thrown in, but Dominick nailed his gaze to Ashlyn.

"Where's Cora?" Dominick immediately asked. "Is she all right?" He went to Ashlyn and reached out for her. The man likely would have grabbed her by the shoulders if Eli hadn't stepped in front of him.

Dominick spared him a glance, one laced with annoyance, before he glared at Ashlyn. "Where is she?" Dominick repeated.

"Cora's fine," Ashlyn answered.

Eli wasn't sure how she managed it, but her voice stayed cool. As did the stare she gave Dominick. She was likely sizing him up, trying to figure out if there was a trace of guilt.

"I want to see her." Dominick made that demand through clenched teeth.

"She's in protective custody," Eli volunteered. "No visitors allowed."

This time Dominick gave him more than just a glance, and the annoyance went up a huge notch. "I'm Cora's grandfather."

"Not legally, and if this is why you wanted to talk to Ashlyn, then you've wasted her time and yours." Eli took hold of her hand, turning as if to leave, and it got the exact reaction he wanted.

"You can't just go," Dominick snapped. "You must know I'm worried sick about my granddaughter being put in danger like that. Gunmen," he spat out like profanity. "It's obvious someone's after Ashlyn, and Cora could get hurt. She'll need more protection than what some local badge can give her."

Eli tapped his badge. "I'm a Texas Ranger, and since both Ashlyn and Cora are unharmed and safe, I think I did an okay job. Plus, I don't have any ulterior motives of trying to get custody of Cora. Unlike you."

Dominick pulled back his shoulders. There was the heat from temper in his expression, but it only lasted a few seconds before the ice came. Oh, yeah. He was capable of hiring thugs to come after Ashlyn.

"Are you suggesting that my client was responsible for the attack?" one of the lawyers snarled.

Eli lifted his shoulder. "If the overly priced shoe fits..."

That brought the other lawyer lurching out of his chair, but with his cold stare still on Eli, Dominick waved the man down after only sparing him a glance. Obviously, Dominick was accustomed to having even his unspoken orders followed.

"I have an alibi for last night," Dominick said, tossing some of that chilly shade on Ashlyn. "Of course, you could say that doesn't matter, that I could have hired those men. But I didn't."

"Can you prove that?" Ashlyn asked, taking the question right out of Eli's mouth. He tried not to beam with pride, but that was some backbone Ashlyn was showing under very difficult circumstances.

Eli hadn't thought the frost in Dominick's eyes could go up any, but he was wrong. It did. "Give the *Texas Ranger* access to my bank account," Dominick snapped, speaking to the lawyers, though this time there wasn't even a glance involved. "That'll prove I didn't hire anyone."

"Thanks for that," Eli said. "But actually it only proves that you didn't use money from the one account that you'll let us examine. It's my guess that a man who wears a suit like yours probably has more than one account."

Eli added a grin that he knew was prime fuel for a hissy fit, which he hoped Dominick would have. Heck, maybe the man would even take a swing at him, and Eli could use the assault to get a warrant to dig even deeper into financials. Goading a possible suspect was a cheap trick, but Eli wasn't above using it to get this man behind bars.

With the pulse throbbing on his throat and his eyes narrowed to slits, Dominick certainly looked as if he wanted to throw a punch, but he finally took a step back. His attention slashed from Eli to Ashlyn.

"You know I wouldn't do anything to harm Cora," Dominick insisted. "I love her."

The love part certainly sounded sincere, but Eli had seen people do all sorts of stupid things in the name of love.

"Do I need to go through a judge to get an order to force you to allow me to see my granddaughter?" Dominick added when Ashlyn didn't say anything.

Ashlyn stared at him for a long moment. "If you truly love her, you won't insist on visiting her when hired guns could follow you to her location. You could put her in danger, and I think any judge will agree with me about that."

"I'd be careful," Dominick blurted out, but then he waved that off. He turned away from them, and

Eli didn't think it was his imagination that the man was grappling with that temper of his that was simmering just beneath the surface.

When Dominick turned back around, he fastened his gaze to Eli. "I don't know if you're good at your job or not, but I am aware that you have a history with Ashlyn."

It didn't surprise Eli that this man had had him investigated, and it only proved what Eli had said to Ashlyn earlier. Dominick could have used their past to put together an attack, one that would be harder to trace back to him.

"I don't think you've looked at all the possible angles about the attack at your house," Dominick added.

"Are you about to tell me that I should be investigating Remy Sager?" Eli came out and asked.

Dominick's glare turned to a frown. Apparently, he wasn't happy that Eli had spoiled his big reveal.

"That's a good start," Dominick grumbled. Now there was some sarcasm in his voice, proving to Eli that the check Dominick had done on Ashlyn and him had gone deep. Of course, Eli hadn't expected anything less. "But you need to look at others, because I believe what happened to Ashlyn and Cora is connected to Marta Seaver's murder."

"Oh?" Eli was pretty sure his sarcasm was better than Dominick's. A small victory, but he didn't like this jerk's attitude.

"Oh," Dominick repeated like profanity. "I know that Leon Taggart is in jail for his part in setting up her murder, but he might have a reach beyond prison bars. You might want to look at Leon's old friend Oscar Cronin."

The name was familiar to Eli. *Very* familiar. Oscar owned a pawnshop, and he had an extremely shady past. That past and his friendship with Leon were the reasons Eli had kept tabs on the man. However, Eli hadn't considered that Oscar would play into this.

"You believe Oscar hired those gunmen on Leon's behalf?" Eli asked.

Dominick shrugged. "I believe that's something you should find out since Oscar's paying regular visits to Leon at the prison."

"I will find out," Eli assured him. "And maybe while I'm checking, I'll ask myself why you just handed me Oscar Cronin on a silver platter. I have a suspicious nature about things like that." He turned to Ashlyn. "Are you ready to go?"

"She can't just leave," Dominick howled. "Not until she's told me where Cora is."

Ashlyn proved the man wrong when she walked out the door with Eli. Dominick might have followed them, but Kellan stepped inside the room, blocking Dominick's way. He then closed the door behind him when he went in to start the official interview.

Eli was about to congratulate Ashlyn for how well she'd held up through that barrage Dominick had doled out to her, but when he felt her shaking, he cursed. Obviously, talking with the idiot had gotten to her after all, because she was pale, too.

"I can't lose Cora," she muttered. "I just can't." And he got the feeling she wasn't just talking about the danger from an attack but also the threat that Dominick could pose.

She went in the direction of the break room but then stopped and ducked into the observation room instead. "I just need a minute to steady myself," she said, her voice suddenly as unsteady as the rest of her.

Eli went in with her. "Don't let him get to you like that."

It was lousy advice, like telling someone not to blink if they heard a loud noise. Ashlyn's fears and concerns were natural, and there wasn't anything he could say to her to soothe that. But apparently his stupid body thought there was something he could *do* in the soothing department, because Eli put his arms around her and eased her to him.

Eli expected her to push him away. She didn't. He expected himself to put a quick end to the hug and curse himself for doing it.

He didn't.

There was some cursing himself involved, but his arms stayed firmly planted around her. From the corner of his eye, he saw Kellan start the interview with Dominick, and Eli considered turning on the audio so he could hear. However, he nixed that idea since he figured it would only add to Ashlyn's shakiness. He'd listen to the recording of the interview once he had Ashlyn and the baby back at the ranch. That way, it would give his own temper a chance to cool down.

"I'm not usually this shaky." Her voice was a whisper. A breathy one. It hit against his neck.

"I'm betting you don't usually have someone kidnap your baby and then try to kill you."

Now he cursed again. And winced. Because obviously someone had tried to kill her in that alley the night Marta had died. Eli braced himself for her to verbally blast him for that, but when she pulled back just enough to meet his gaze, there was no blasting involved.

Hell.

There was plenty of heat, though. It was masked a little behind her worried and somewhat confused expression, but it was there. And for one bad moment, he got a flashback. Not the kind that came from being a lawman. This one was of her nearly naked and cuddled up with him on the seat of his truck.

"Thanks," she said, her voice still a whisper. Yeah, the breath was there, too, but this time it landed against his mouth. She noticed it, too, because she pulled back even farther. "Sorry. Sometimes I forget why that's a bad idea. Then I get an old picture of us in my head, and I remember."

"In a memory contest, I bet I would win."

Of course, the moment the words came out, he wanted to hit himself, but he decided just to own the stupid remark. Eli gave her as much of a smile as he could manage. It wasn't a good one, but it seemed to be enough to stop her from trembling. It even gave her a little bit of color in her cheeks.

"Thanks," she repeated, but this time her tone had something they both wanted. Awkwardness. It was a hell of a lot better than his remembering how she looked naked.

Or wanting to kiss her.

Ashlyn dragged in a deep breath, pulled back her shoulders. "So, was Dominick trying to muddy things by bringing up Leon and Oscar?"

It was a good question, the right one to diffuse this restless energy between them, and it helped Eli get his thoughts back where they belonged. "Maybe. I'll talk to the warden at the prison and see what I can find out. Unless Leon's come into some money lately like Remy, then he hasn't got the funds to hire two guns. I don't know anything about Oscar—yet."

And speaking of Remy, that was Eli's cue to see if the man had arrived yet. That would also put some distance between Ashlyn and him. "I need to talk to Owen. After that, Gunnar and I can drive Cora and you back to the ranch."

She glanced at Dominick, who appeared to be in the same riled mood he was when Ashlyn was in the room with him, and she shook her head. "I'll listen to Dominick, and then we can go."

Eli didn't think the listening part was a good idea, because it would likely upset her, but he couldn't blame her. If he were in her shoes, he'd want to know every possible aspect of the investigation. He flicked on the switch for the audio and went in search of Owen. He wouldn't dawdle, though, because the memory of Ashlyn trembling was still way too fresh in his mind.

When Eli made it to the bullpen, he glanced around and soon spotted Owen. "Any sign of Remy?"

"Not yet. He called to say he was delayed because he's waiting on his lawyer. He'll be here in about an hour."

An hour was going to feel like an eternity with Cora in the break room and Dominick just up the hall. Eli knew it was stupid for him to feel as if he had such high emotional stakes when it came to the baby. But he did.

"I'll call Remy and tell him to get his butt in here ASAP," Eli grumbled. And if not, he'd see about getting a warrant for his arrest. Remy ticked all the boxes when it came to suspects, and Eli didn't want the man dodging them while he came up with an alibi or a way to escape justice.

"Hold off on that call," Owen said, his attention on the screen of his desk computer. "I just got a report from SAPD." Owen looked up at him. "They sent an officer out to talk to the mortician who works at the funeral home that handled Marta's remains."

"Terrell Wilburn," Eli supplied. He didn't like that suddenly tight look on his brother's face. "And what did he have to say?"

"He's dead." Owen's tense look only got worse. "Someone murdered him yesterday afternoon. A gunshot wound to the head."

Eli felt the shock of that ram straight into him. He doubted it was a coincidence that the mortician had died just hours before the kidnapping and the attack.

"Who killed him?" Eli asked.

"SAPD doesn't know yet. There's more," Owen quickly added. "The killer apparently stole Wilburn's laptop, but Wilburn had some hard copy files in his office. There was a folder with Marta's name on it."

"And?" Eli prompted when Owen paused.

"It was empty," Owen said. "It looks as if the killer took whatever was in it."

Chapter Seven

Ashlyn listened to every word of Dominick's interview. Of course, he claimed he was innocent of hiring the gunmen. And maybe he was. But she had no intention of letting him see Cora until they had the person responsible for the attack behind bars.

Whenever that would be.

It sickened her to think that the search could go on for days, weeks or even longer, but she had to hold on to the hope that maybe there wouldn't be another attack. That whoever was behind this was done. But she had to be sure. For the sake of her baby, she needed to be certain that no one else would come after them.

After Dominick and his lawyers were gone, Ashlyn went into the break room to check on Cora. She was asleep in Gloria's arms, and Owen was still standing guard. Seeing both steadied her nerves a little so she went in search of Eli so she could find out when they'd be going back to Jack's place. Not that Ashlyn especially wanted to go there, but she didn't like the alternative of staying in the sheriff's office where Dominick could return.

She coiled her way around the hall and spotted Eli in Kellan's office. The two were huddled over a computer, and judging from their stern expressions, something hadn't gone the way they wanted. When she stepped in, both men looked at her, but then Kellan gave Eli a nod. Obviously, that was a cue for Eli to fill her in. The fact that he had to take a deep breath first told her that she wasn't going to like this much, either.

"Someone murdered the mortician who handled Marta's remains. They stole his file on her and his computer." Eli said it quickly and continued before she could do anything more than gasp. "We're starting the paperwork to have Marta's remains exhumed."

Ashlyn still didn't manage more than a gasp, but she did make her way to the chair to sit. Her legs suddenly didn't feel very steady. Someone was dead. Someone connected to all of this.

"There's no concrete proof that Marta didn't die the night of her attack," Kellan added, "but we need to be sure."

Yes, they did. And a few minutes ago, Ashlyn would have insisted that she needed no such proof as seeing her friend's body. But now with the mortician's murder, it was something that had to be investigated.

The memories of Marta's murder came, of course, and like always they were smeared together with the pain of her own shooting. With the anger and betrayal she felt about Eli. But that had changed, too, she realized.

Everything had changed.

"Why would Marta have faked her death?" Ashlyn asked when some of the numbing shock finally wore off.

"Maybe she wasn't the one who did it," Eli said, but his attention wasn't on her. It was on the front door, and she followed his gaze to the man who'd just stepped in.

Remy.

She wanted to ask why Remy, or anyone else for that matter, would do something like that, but Remy spotted them, too, and he made a beeline toward them.

Ashlyn stood, steeling herself up for what would no doubt be an onslaught of anger fueled by grief. Until today, she'd understood that, but now she looked at Remy as someone who might have tried to murder Eli and her.

Had he actually done that?

She studied him as he stormed closer. Tall with black hair and dark brown eyes. Attractive in a bad-boy sort of way. A way that had certainly appealed to Marta. Even after Marta had turned her life around and gone straight, she'd kept that thing she had for bad boys.

"I don't appreciate getting a threat about being arrested." Remy aimed that snarl at Eli. "My lawyer still hasn't shown up."

"Then get him here right now because you've had more than enough time," Eli fired back, and his snarl was harder than Remy's. "We've got questions, and you're going to give us those answers."

Remy flickered an annoyed glance at Ashlyn. This time, she saw the blame he sent her way. Blame for what Remy saw as her part in not preventing Marta's death. Or at least that's what she thought it was, but maybe it was all an act. Because maybe Marta wasn't actually dead.

"Yeah, yeah," Remy grumbled to Eli once his gaze was back on him. "Somebody tried to off you, and you're looking to pin it on me."

"I'm looking for the truth," Eli assured him. "I heard you inherited some money, and once your lawyer's here, I'll want to ask you some questions about how you might have used those funds. After all, hired guns cost big bucks."

Remy gave him an arctic stare. "I didn't do that, and you've got no proof that I did."

Eli lifted his shoulder. "I'll be pressing you more about that—again when your lawyer gets here. And after you've cleared up that matter, I'll want to know if you helped Marta fake her death."

Remy had already turned to leave, but that stopped him in his tracks. "What did you say?"

"You lawyered up," Eli reminded him, and yes, there was some cocky smugness in his tone and expression. "I can't talk to you about that until he or she gets here."

Remy's glare vanished, replaced by some confusion. He frantically shook his head. "Marta faked her death?" That certainly didn't seem like old news to him. His eyes were wide now, and his mouth was slightly open.

"You lawyered up," Eli repeated.

"To hell with the lawyer." Remy practically knocked into her when he rushed toward the desk where Eli was standing. "Is Marta alive?" He volleyed glances at all three of them while he repeated the question.

"Are you waiving your right to counsel?" Kellan clarified.

"Yes!" Remy snapped. "Now tell me about Marta."

Kellan read the man his rights first, and with each word of the Miranda warning, Remy's impatience skyrocketed. "Is she alive?" Remy shouted.

"We don't know. That's the truth," Eli added when Remy looked ready to yell again. "Someone stole her records and murdered the mortician who handled her remains. Tell me what you know about that."

Remy dropped back a step, and he pressed his hand to his chest. "Nothing. I don't know anything about it." He dragged in some rough breaths, and his gaze slashed to Ashlyn. "You saw her dead. You told me you saw her dead."

"I did." Of course, now Ashlyn had to wonder if what she'd seen was true.

"I felt for a pulse," Eli went on, "and she didn't have one. Marta was dead at the scene. I'd bet my badge on that."

Remy shook his head. "But what about the missing records? What about the dead mortician? Does that mean someone wanted to cover up that she's actually alive?"

"No," Eli quickly answered. "They could be just smoke screens." He paused a heartbeat. "Tell me about the disagreement you had with Marta's family about where she was to be buried."

Remy blinked, obviously not expecting that to come up. "Uh, her dad, Gus, wanted to bury her in Oklahoma. I wanted her buried in San Antonio so I could visit her grave. Marta would have wanted that, too," Remy quickly clarified, "but Gus wouldn't bend. He put her in the ground in a place she didn't want to be."

Some of the shock was gone now, and in its place was some venom and bitterness.

"Did that rile you enough to play mind games?" Eli pressed. "Mind games that include getting back at Ashlyn and me?"

Remy's eyes were narrowed when they came back

to Eli. "No. I told you I didn't try to kill you. Even though you both deserve it," he added in a grumble. "You let Marta die in that alley, and now you're on a witch hunt to add more misery to my life."

"No witch hunt," Eli tried to assure him, but Remy interrupted him.

"Was it one of you who broke in to my house?" Remy demanded.

Ashlyn sighed. "No," she insisted, but Eli only tapped his badge to remind Remy that he was the law, not the criminal.

Remy didn't look as if he believed them. "Well, somebody broke in night before last and stole my laptop and cell phone. I got a new phone with the same number, but I didn't have all my computer files backed up online."

That got her attention. Eli had said the mortician's computer and files had been stolen, too. She didn't know the timing of that, but she had to wonder if it was connected to the break-in at Remy's. Of course, Remy could be lying about that.

"Now you demand I come in for questioning and tell me stuff about Marta," Remy went on. "What the hell am I supposed to think?" But he waved that off. "I've changed my mind. I'll wait for my lawyer. I won't say anything else until he gets here."

"Suit yourself." Kellan tipped his head toward the hall. "Come with me. You can wait in the interview room."

Ashlyn watched them leave and waited until they were out of sight before she turned to Eli. "You believe him?" she asked.

Eli rubbed his hand over his forehead. "I'm not sure. He hates both of us, and I don't know how far he'd take that hate."

Neither did she. But maybe they could find out. "I can call some of Marta's old friends and find out if they've noticed anything off about Remy. I'll need my cell phone for that, though, because it has the contact numbers. It's still at my house. I didn't bring it with me when I went looking for Cora."

He nodded. "Calling her friends is a good idea, but don't mention the fake death theory to any of them just yet. I want to talk to Marta's dad first."

Just hearing that caused her stomach to twist. Unlike Remy, Marta's father hadn't held the anger and hatred for them, but he had been torn up by his daughter's murder. She doubted that grief had gone away even after all these months.

"The CSIs are done processing our houses," Eli told her. "I got word about that right after I left the observation room." His gaze came to hers. Lingering. And reminding her of what had happened between them there.

A hug.

She might be able to convince herself it had only been that. Might. But she couldn't do much convincing with Eli giving her that smoldering look.

Ashlyn cleared her throat, glanced away. "I'll need to drop by my house and check on my horses and the ones I board. I could get my cell phone and some of my things while I'm there." She paused, gave that some thought. Actually, a lot of thought. "I don't feel comfortable taking Cora back there just yet."

"Because you're smart, that's why. It's not safe. If there are more hired guns, your house and mine would be the first places they'd go. I'll take you to your house later today. *With backup*," he emphasized. "It'll have to be a quick in and out, and we won't be taking Cora with us. She can stay at Jack's with Gloria and a couple of the deputies."

Good. She hated the idea of leaving her baby, but she would hate it even more if Cora was with them during another attack. And Eli was right. If there were other gunmen, her house would be a prime target.

"I'll call Gus now," Eli said, taking out his phone.

With her breath held, she watched as Eli located Gus Seaver's number, and after he put his phone on speaker, he tried the call. No answer. When it went to voice mail, Eli left a message for the man to contact him. Eli had barely finished it when Gunnar stepped through the door.

"Remy's lawyer is here," Gunnar said, "and so is a guy named Oscar Cronin. He wants to see you. He says he's a friend of Leon Taggart."

Eli and she exchanged surprised glances. She

definitely hadn't expected Oscar to come to them, though she was certain Eli would have gotten around to getting in touch with the man.

"Check Oscar for weapons," Eli instructed, causing her heart rate to spike. She hadn't considered that he'd come here to attack them, but she should have. She should be thinking worst-case scenario right now so she could make sure Cora stayed safe.

"Move over here," Eli told her after Gunnar had left, and he motioned for her to come behind the desk. Once she'd done that, he positioned himself in front of her, and he put his hand on the gun in his holster.

Maybe it was Eli's stance, but it caused the wiry, gray-haired man to come to a stop in the doorway. She'd never met Oscar, but as Ashlyn studied him, she realized she'd seen him in court when Leon had entered his plea before the judge. Oscar was about the same age as Leon, late forties, but he was a good foot shorter than Leon. She'd always thought Leon looked like a criminal. Oscar certainly didn't, and his pale complexion and the cough that rattled in his chest made her think that he might not be in the best of health.

"Sergeant Slater. Miss Darrow," he greeted, and it wasn't a question. Obviously, he recognized them, too. "I heard about the trouble y'all had last night and figured you'd want to talk to me."

Eli just stared at him, and even though Ashlyn couldn't see Eli's face, she was betting one of his eyebrows was raised. "Why, did you have something to do with that?"

Oscar gave a dry smile, shook his head. "Dominick called me early this morning and said he intended to mention me in an interview. I thought I'd save you the trouble by coming here and letting you know I didn't try to kill either one of you."

Normally, Ashlyn would have liked his direct approach, but she wasn't about to trust this man. "How do you know Dominick?" she asked.

"That's just it—I don't. He called me out of the blue, claimed he was looking into your background, and he wanted to know if I could tell him anything."

"Anything?" Eli snapped. "What specifically?"

"Didn't say, and I didn't ask. That's because I told him I didn't know Miss Darrow. Or you," he added to Eli. "Because he asked about you, too."

Ashlyn wanted to groan. Dominick was digging for dirt, probably so he could find something to use against her in a custody fight, and he would have gone to Oscar because of his connection to Marta and Leon.

"I figure this Dominick might be trying to set me up for something," Oscar went on. He coughed again. "I mean, why else would he call me and say he was going to mention me in an interview with a cop and Texas Ranger?"

"Good question," Eli said. "Why do *you* think Dominick would do that?"

Oscar lifted his shoulder. "I'm an easy target. I'm dying," Oscar added without any change in his tone. "Lung cancer. I'm home alone a lot with no alibis. Maybe someone like Dominick wants to do something bad—like go after the two of you—and then blame me for it. Whatever he's up to, I'm thinking it's no good."

Ashlyn thought the same thing. However, she could see this from a different angle. Leon and Oscar were friends, and maybe with Oscar dying, he wouldn't mind doing his old friend a favor by getting back at the two people who helped put him behind bars.

"I heard the deputy say that Remy's lawyer was here," Oscar went on. "I guess it doesn't surprise me that Remy would be a suspect in this, too."

"You know Remy?" Eli asked.

"Of course. And Marta," he readily admitted. Then he paused. "I've been hearing things lately. Rumors. They've got to be rumors," Oscar added as if talking to himself.

Eli kept his attention nailed to the man. "What have you heard?"

Oscar opened his mouth. Closed it. And he seemed to reconsider what he'd been about to say. "Leon's no threat to anybody. The man doesn't have a nickel to his name. But there could be other folks out there, drug dealers, who might not be pleased that Marta was tattling on them to the cops."

Everything inside Ashlyn went still. "What are you talking about?"

"Marta." That's all Oscar said for several long moments. "The rumors I've heard are that she's alive, that she faked her death to hide out from some of those dealers who might want her dead for real. If that's true, give her some advice from me. She'd better stay dead."

Chapter Eight

There was a whole lot of information—and questions—going through Eli's head. He'd thought that
being at Jack's house would help him process all
of it since it was quieter here than it'd been at the
sheriff's office. But the processing just kept circling
back to one of the questions.

Was Marta actually alive?

If she was, did that have anything to do with the
attack and the mortician's murder?

No matter how it circled and mentally played
out, Eli just couldn't see Marta faking her death
and letting everyone believe she'd been murdered.
Nor could he see Marta killing anyone, but maybe
someone had done it on her behalf. Someone like
Remy, who wanted to protect her from drug dealers who might come after her if they found out she
was alive. But Remy had looked shocked when Eli
had brought up the possibility of Marta surviving
the shooting.

Real shock.

It was hard to fake that. Then again, the surprise could have been simply because Remy hadn't expected Eli to know anything about it.

While standing by the kitchen table, Eli drank more coffee, studied his notes on his laptop and then glanced at his phone. He considered giving Marta's father another call, but before he could do that, Ashlyn came into the kitchen. She looked exhausted with her pale face, heavy-lidded eyes and rumpled hair. Those were the first things he noticed. The second thing that snagged his attention was that despite the fatigue, she looked good.

Hell.

He might as well hit his head against the wall a couple of times. He'd known that hug in the observation room was a mistake, but Eli hadn't counted on it lighting a couple more fires that shouldn't be lit.

She glanced at Gunnar, who was grabbing a catnap on the sofa. "Cora's finally asleep," she whispered to Eli. She went to the fridge and got a bottle of water. "Gloria's with her."

Not a surprise, since Gloria hadn't left the baby's side since they'd arrived. That was good, and Eli hoped the woman continued to be okay with that arrangement since she might be there for a while.

"I'll text Owen and tell him to come so he can stay here while Gunnar, you and I go out to your place," Eli offered, and he fired off the message. "Or if you're having second thoughts about going, I can get the things you need and bring them to you. You could make a list."

She shook her head. "I want to make sure the horses are okay." Then she paused. "I want to make sure I'm okay, too. I need to be able to go back there, to prove to myself that I can do it."

Eli understood that. It was akin to getting back on a horse that'd just thrown you. But the horse wasn't going to hire gunmen to kill you.

"It's my home," Ashlyn added as if she needed to convince him, but it sounded as if she was actually trying to convince herself. "If I can't stay there, then…well, it changes everything."

Yeah. She'd have to sell the house and land that'd been in her family for a couple of generations. She would have to give up her livelihood, too, at least until she found another place big enough for the horses.

He hadn't thought it possible, but Ashlyn now looked even more exhausted than she had when she'd first come into the kitchen. Eli wished there was something he could do to help with that. Of course, his stupid body came up with a few bad suggestions, but he shoved them aside. Holding and kissing her wasn't going to help.

"You scowl whenever I'm around," she said, and

Ashlyn reached up and touched her fingers to the muscles that were bunched up there.

Eli probably should have just blown that off and gotten the conversation back on the right track. He could do that easily by telling her the bits and pieces of info he'd learned about the investigation. But apparently, this was going to be the day his brain joined the other stupid parts of him.

"Naked thoughts," he admitted.

Her eyebrow rose. "Of us." Now she got some color when she blushed. "Of us in your truck," she continued without waiting for him to say anything. "It's firm in my memory because you were my first. That creates a strange intimacy. A connection. No matter what happens afterward, it stays with a woman."

"It stays with a man, too." Apparently, the stupidity was just going to keep on coming from him.

The corner of her mouth lifted for a quick smile. "I wasn't your first," she pointed out.

He nearly blurted out that some were more memorable than others. Ashlyn had definitely been memorable. But he'd filled his dumb things to say quota for the day.

"Losing you was hard," she went on. "Then, hating you for Marta…" She stopped, waved it off.

Eli just stared at her and waited her out. It took her several moments, and she kept her gaze on the floor, but Ashlyn finally continued. "This might be easier if I really did hate you. I don't." She looked up at him, and yeah, their eyes locked.

"It wouldn't be easier," he assured her. "I didn't like you hating me."

She gave him that half smile again and brushed her hand down his arm. It wasn't a flirty kind of gesture. More the signaling of some kind of truce.

Despite that, it went straight to his groin.

That wasn't a good direction for any kind of feeling to go, and before Eli could talk some sense into himself, he slipped his hand around the back of Ashlyn's neck, pulled her to him and kissed her.

Eli grimaced at her taste. Not because it was bad but because it was damn good. Like a really nice present that he'd just unwrapped. A hot one, and that heat did a number on him when it slid right through him.

Ashlyn moaned, her pleasure mixed with some hesitation. Which meant she was smarter than he was right now because he couldn't muster up any hesitation whatsoever. None. Eli just hauled her closer and deepened the kiss until it was more than a mere slide of heat. There was need. An urgency. The kind of rush that upped the stupidity and made him remember being naked with her in his truck.

Gunnar's noisy yawn caused them to jerk apart—which Eli was certain he should see as a good thing. Once his body softened and the steam cleared in his head, that is. Gunnar lifted his head, glancing at them from over the back of the sofa. In that glance Eli got a reminder that Gunnar was a good cop, because he saw the realization in the deputy's eyes. Gunnar knew what they'd been doing.

"I'll be back," Gunnar mumbled, tipping his head in the general direction of the hall bathroom. That was no doubt an invitation for Ashlyn and him to continue the mistake they'd just been making. They wouldn't. But Eli figured he'd be thinking way too much about doing it again.

"I know you're sorry that happened," Ashlyn whispered. "There's no need to apologize."

She didn't give him a chance to even consider if he wanted to do that. Ashlyn went back to the fridge and took out one of the sandwiches that they'd picked up earlier from the diner. Apparently, kissing him made her hungry. He was hungry, all right, but not for food.

"Were you able to find out any more about Dominick's bank account?" she asked.

He reminded himself that talking about the investigation was a good thing. Whether it felt like one or not. "Nothing. No suspicious withdrawals." Of course, Eli hadn't expected there to be, since Dominick had voluntarily given them access. "I called the prison, and the warden is setting up a phone call with Leon. I want to ask him about Oscar, about what he said."

She nodded. "It's true that Oscar visited Leon?"

"Yes. He's been there three times since Leon's conviction, but two of those visits have happened in the last month. The conversations were monitored, but the recordings of the visits have already been wiped."

Judging from her expression, she wasn't any more pleased with the timing than Eli was. He was about to add that maybe they would get Leon to tell them what Oscar and he had discussed during those visits, but there was still way too much fog and heat cluttering his mind.

"Look, I just want to get this off my chest," he grumbled. "I didn't kiss you so that you'd stop hating me. Or so you'd stop feeling as if I didn't do my job the night Marta and you were shot. The kiss just happened."

He wanted to groan because that sounded about as stupid as the kiss itself had been. The fact that it was true didn't make it better.

She took in a breath and stared at him as if considering that. "I didn't think that. It didn't seem like some kind of ploy or test. It felt like, well, like what it actually was—lust." She glanced in the direction of his zipper and actually managed a smile.

That didn't make it better, either, but Eli found himself wanting to smile, too. Thankfully, he was spared from doing that because his phone rang. Not the prison, but it was a call he'd been expecting.

"It's Marta's dad," Eli let her know, and he took

the call on speaker so that Ashlyn would be able to hear.

"Sergeant Slater," Gus greeted. "I didn't expect to hear from you."

And he didn't sound especially happy about it. Eli couldn't blame the man. Just hearing Eli's voice likely brought back a slew of bad memories. Eli figured that would only get worse with this call.

"Some questions have come up," Eli started. There was no easy way to say this so he just put it out there as fast as he could. "The mortician who handled your daughter's remains has been murdered. Marta's file was stolen. Her hospital records are missing. All of that doesn't add up to a solid conclusion, but I have to ask the question. Do you believe Marta's still alive?"

Silence. For a long time. "Is this some kind of sick joke?" Gus finally snapped.

"No," Eli assured him. "Do you believe she's alive?" he repeated.

"Of course not. I buried her. You know that."

Yes, he thought he did. Eli had gone to the funeral, but it'd been a closed-casket service. "Did you actually see Marta's body?"

"No, but—" There was another stretch of silence. "Tell me straight what's going on," Gus demanded.

Because he figured he would need it, Eli first drew in a long breath. "Like I said, what I have isn't close to being conclusive. A mortician's dead, files are missing, and I had a person come forward who claims to have heard rumors that Marta might have faked her death to hide from some drug dealers. I just need to know if you think there's any chance that happened."

There was another long silence. "I didn't ask to see her body. I couldn't."

Eli got that, but he wished that Gus had taken a glimpse of his daughter when he'd said goodbye. "I've done the paperwork to exhume Marta's body." Eli paused long enough to give the man time to object.

Gus didn't.

"You really think she could be alive?" Gus asked, and Eli hated the hope that he heard in the man's voice.

"I have to rule it out," Eli settled for saying.

"Then get it done. In fact, if it'll speed things along, I'll pay for it. I want it done immediately."

Eli wasn't sure he could make *immediately* happen, but he could press. "I'll see what I can do," he assured Gus, and he ended the call so that he could message Kellan to get him involved.

When he finished the text, Eli saw that Gus wasn't the only one with some hope. Ashlyn had it, too. Hell, so did he. But if Marta was alive, then it was going to pose a whole new problem for them. Such as—had Marta had any involvement in the attack from the hired guns?

Before Eli could give that any thought, his phone rang again, and this time it was the prison. As he'd done with Gus, he put the call on speaker, and after several transfers, he finally heard the familiar voice.

"Sergeant Slater," Leon greeted. His voice was low and raspy. "Long time, no see. You're alive and kicking, I guess?"

"Any reason I wouldn't be?" Eli countered, and he tried to make the muscles in his chest relax. Hard to do since this was the man who'd orchestrated an ambush that had killed one person and wounded Ashlyn.

Well, wounded Ashlyn, anyway.

With what he was hearing about Marta, he might have to amend Leon's label. His lawyers would want an amendment, too, and if Marta was truly alive, they could use that to get Leon a much reduced sentence.

"I heard about the trouble you had out at your place," Leon answered. "Lots of gossip about it, and it was on the news. The details are a little sketchy, but it sounds like someone took some shots at you."

Eli didn't doubt the news or gossip part, but that might not have been the reason Leon knew about it. He might have firsthand knowledge. "You're sure you didn't hire someone to kill me?"

Leon laughed. "You have access to my bank accounts. Oh, wait. I don't have any bank accounts because I don't have any money. You also have access to any and all of my visits so unless you think my lawyer floated me a loan, then you know I didn't hire anyone."

Yes, Eli did have access to those things, but that didn't mean something couldn't slip by. "You hate me. That means you might have found a way to come after me."

No laugh this time, but there was a heavy sigh. "I don't want you dead. Didn't want you dead that night, either. Drake said he needed to have it out with Marta, that he was going to convince her to quit ratting on him. You and Marta's friend, Ashlyn, were just in the wrong place at the wrong time."

Ashlyn went a little pale again, and she was no doubt battling the flashbacks from that night.

"So you didn't want me dead, only Marta?" Eli said.

"Didn't want Marta dead, either," Leon insisted. "I actually liked her, but Drake was paying, and I needed cash. It wasn't personal, just business."

There was no chance of Eli's chest muscles relaxing with that. He wanted to reach through the phone and beat Leon senseless. "It was personal to me," Eli said, his voice a low, dangerous warning.

Leon stayed quiet a moment. "What's this call all about? Because I doubt you're just wanting a trip down that particular memory lane."

"It's about Oscar. Tell me about his visits."

"Oscar," Leon repeated, and he didn't sound surprised. More like resigned that his old friend was going to come up in conversation. "You think he's the one who hired the gunmen."

"Did he?" Eli pressed.

Leon gave another sigh. "Maybe. I honestly don't know for sure," he quickly added before Eli could challenge his answer. "Unlike me, what happened with Drake is personal."

Everything inside Eli went still. "Explain that."

"Oscar and Drake were like brothers, and Oscar wasn't happy when you killed Drake."

"Well, I wasn't happy when Drake gunned down Marta, shot Ashlyn and then tried to kill me. I get testy when things like that happen. What the hell did Oscar say to you when he visited you in prison?" Eli demanded.

"That he wasn't happy about some honor that you got," Leon answered after a short hesitation. "He got all worked up when you got a commendation last month."

Eli had indeed gotten that, because he'd tracked down a killer and saved the hostage that the killer had taken. The commendation had embarrassed him some since he'd just been doing his job, and now it had had this effect. But Eli hadn't seen anything "worked up" about Oscar when he'd come into the sheriff's office.

"Oscar was angry about that?" Eli pressed.

"Yeah, he said he didn't like that you were getting on with your life when you'd cut Drake's life short. And there's no need for you to remind me that Drake was trying to kill you. Oscar doesn't believe that. Oh, and he's riled about Ashlyn, too."

Ashlyn's eyes widened. "Why?" she asked.

"Because Oscar heard you'd adopted a kid." Obviously, Leon wasn't surprised that Ashlyn had been listening to their conversation. "It's that whole getting on with your life thing." He paused again. "Look, I think Oscar would like it better if you two were wallowing in grief over what happened."

Maybe they weren't exactly wallowing, but it was still haunting them. Worse, it could be the reason for the attack.

"Why did Oscar come to visit you twice in the past month?" Eli went on.

Leon groaned but also made a sound of dismissal. "He just wanted to rant, that's all. He went on and on about Ashlyn's kid and your medal. I told him to cool off, but it didn't help much. He hates your guts."

"That's it?" Eli didn't roll his eyes, but that's what he wanted to do. "He drove all that way there just to vent?"

"That and he wanted to know if I'd kept in touch with any of my old friends."

Eli got that feeling down his spine, the one that told him that he was finally onto something. "What old friends?"

"Just some guys I used to hang out with." Leon's tone was casual, but there was nothing casual about what Eli was feeling, and it wasn't a feeling he intended to push aside.

"Are you talking about criminal friends?" Eli pressed.

"They've got records, yeah, but Oscar said he might needs some help at his pawnshop. I took that to mean he might need a little muscle or something like that. Maybe some protection in case he'd made some deals that could cause him problems."

"Criminal friends," Eli flatly repeated. "Were two of those guys Charles Cardona and Abe Franklin?" Eli didn't explain that those were the names of the two dead gunmen who'd tried to kill Ashlyn and him. He just waited for Leon to respond, and it didn't take long.

Leon cursed. "I think it's time I called my lawyer."

And with that, Leon ended the call.

Chapter Nine

Ashlyn listened as Eli made the follow-up calls about Oscar and Leon. Calls that might hopefully link Oscar to the attack. Of course, Leon had already linked the man by what he'd told Eli and her, but they would need more than the hearsay of a convict to consider Oscar a real suspect.

Eli was just finishing up those calls when Owen and another deputy, Raylene McNeal, arrived. Ashlyn hadn't expected the second backup, but she was pleased about it. They had the ranch hands keeping an eye on the place, but she preferred having two trained law enforcement officers guarding her daughter while Eli and she were at her place.

"Oscar's not answering his phone. It went straight to voice mail," Eli told her, and he filled in his brother, Gunnar and Raylene while Ashlyn did a quick check on Cora to make sure she was still asleep.

She was.

Maybe they could make it back from her house before the baby woke up. Then she could spend some time with her while she helped Eli unravel this thread that Leon had given them.

When she went back into the living room, Gunnar and Eli were already at the door. Owen, too, and she heard him lock the door as soon as Gunnar, Eli and she were out and heading to the cruiser.

"Is there any reason for Leon to lie about this?" Gunnar asked once they were inside. It was a good question and something that Ashlyn was already considering.

"Maybe Leon's just ticked off at Oscar about something and thought this was the way to get back at him." Then Eli shook his head. "But if that were true, Leon would have already figured out a way to get in touch with me so he could blab. What he told us felt more spur-of-the-moment."

Ashlyn made a sound of agreement. "And Leon's worried that he could be considered an accessory after the fact for the attack."

That got nods from both Gunnar and Eli, and while she knew they'd heard every word she'd said, they both had their attention on their surroundings. It was all rural property between her place and the Slater ranch, which meant there were plenty of places for a hired gun to lie in wait.

"When SAPD and the Rangers were investigating Marta's murder, nothing came up about a connection between Drake and Oscar?" Gunnar asked. He was behind the wheel, and he made brief eye contact with Eli in the rearview mirror.

"Oscar was interviewed, but so were nearly a hundred others." Eli cursed under his breath. "It was a connection I should have made."

Ashlyn huffed to let him know that there was no way he should put this on his shoulders, and then she realized the huff was a sympathetic show of support. Something Eli wouldn't want. Something that was a by-product of the kiss in the kitchen.

A kiss that had changed everything.

Actually, the change had started before that, around about the time she'd realized they were in this together and that they needed to trust each other. But the kiss had sealed the deal, and no matter how Ashlyn spun it in her head, it had reminded her of a man—or rather a boy—that she'd once loved enough for him to be her first.

Now she wanted him all over again.

She huffed again at that, causing Eli to look at her. Gunnar gave her a glance in the mirror, but thankfully she didn't have to explain herself because Gunnar took the final turn to her place.

Ashlyn automatically moved closer to the window when her house came into view. Before the attack, there'd been only good memories here, but now she could hear the sounds of those gunmen. Feel the hit from the stun gun. And the terror. Most of all, she remembered the absolute terror of them taking Cora.

She jolted when Eli slipped his hand over hers. Obviously, she was past being just on edge. Ashlyn had never had a panic attack before, but she was worried that it might happen now.

"We don't have to do this," Eli said, his voice a soothing whisper. She wanted to latch onto it. Onto him. So she gripped his hand harder and steeled herself.

"I hate them," she murmured. "The gunmen. Even though they're dead, I hate them for bringing this to my home." She shook her head to try to clear it. "I won't let them take this away from me."

"Good." Eli's voice wasn't so soothing now. "Don't let the SOBs take away anything from you. You're tough. Hell, you survived getting shot. And you can get through this."

She looked at him to see if it was lip service. But it wasn't. She could tell that from his fierce expression and his eyes. Ashlyn was about to say he was wrong, that she wasn't tough, but she re-thought that. She would do anything—anything—to keep her daughter safe, so that meant she could get through this.

Gunnar pulled to a stop in front of her house and looked back at Eli and her. "Why don't I check on the horses? I can make sure they're fed and have water. Ashlyn, you can pack the things you need."

Considering that Eli agreed so quickly, it meant Gunnar and he had likely already worked this out so that she'd be in the house and not out in the open. Ashlyn didn't argue, but she hoped she got at least glimpses of the horses so she could see for herself that they were okay.

Just as they'd done the other times at Jack's house, Eli moved her fast from the cruiser to her front door—after Gunnar had already opened it. She was outside for only a couple of seconds while both Eli and Gunnar protected her. Ashlyn hated that they had to put their lives on the line for her like that, but maybe they'd get answers soon so that Eli could make an arrest.

Gunnar did a quick check of the house, something that sent her heart pounding because it was a reminder that someone could have broken in. Someone who might be still be there and was lying in wait for them.

But nothing, thank goodness.

Once he'd finished his search, Gunnar went straight out the back door, hurrying, no doubt so he could finish the chores and get them out of there fast. Ashlyn headed to her bedroom and tried not to focus on the signs of what had been a struggle between her and the gunmen. A broken lamp and toppled furniture.

Eli stayed right next to her as she walked down

the hall, but he stopped in the doorway of her bedroom when his phone dinged with a message.

"We got the approval we needed to exhume Marta's body," Eli relayed to her. "They'll start digging soon."

Which meant that it wouldn't be long before they had answers. If Marta was truly alive, then that would start a whole new investigation.

She grabbed a suitcase from her closet and stuffed in some clothes and then went into the adjoining bathroom to do the same with her toiletries and meds. When she came back out, she saw Eli glancing at the books on her nightstand while he kept watch at the window.

"Parenting books," she explained, though Eli could easily tell that from the titles. "I wanted to do everything right. I didn't want to take a chance of messing it up. It's the most important thing I've ever done."

Eli didn't seem surprised by that. Probably because even in high school she'd mentioned that someday she wanted kids.

"I've seen how you are with Cora, and you're a great mom," he said, his glance going to her this time.

Ashlyn wasn't sure why that felt like such high praise coming from him. And then she remembered something else. "You wanted kids, too." But the moment the words left her mouth, she winced. After that kiss, he might think she was trying to thrust both a relationship and fatherhood on him. "Sorry. That didn't sound right."

He lifted his shoulder and seemed more, well, amused than manipulated. The expression didn't last long, though. His forehead bunched up, and he hurried out of the room.

"Stay away from the windows," Eli warned her as he ran.

The chill rippled over her skin, and just like that, her heart began to pound. With her suitcase gripped in her hand, Ashlyn followed Eli and saw him in the kitchen. She didn't go closer because there was a wall of windows above the sink and counter, and from those windows, she had a clear view of the barn.

"What's wrong?" she asked once she had gathered enough breath to speak.

Eli didn't jump to answer, and he continued to fire his gaze around the yard and barn. "Maybe nothing. I thought I saw someone, but I could be wrong."

She wanted to believe that. Ashlyn wanted to latch onto it so she could try to tamp down the nerves that were now raw and hot.

"I'm texting Gunnar to have him come back inside," Eli added a moment later. "We're leaving."

Good. She didn't want to be there if there was some kind of danger, and she set down her suitcase, waiting to find out what was going on.

Eli took out his phone, but he didn't manage to send the text before the bullet came crashing through the window.

ELI DIDN'T SEE the shot coming, but he sure as hell heard it. And he felt it.

The glass exploded, sending sharp pieces right at him, and he felt one of those pieces slice across his sleeve and arm. There was a quick jolt of pain, which he ignored, because he lunged at Ashlyn, pulling her to the floor with him.

They fell hard, causing Eli to see stars when he crashed onto the floor. Not a second too soon. Because another bullet bashed through the window and into the kitchen.

"Gunnar," Ashlyn said on a rise of breath.

Yeah, Eli hadn't forgotten about the deputy and hoped like the devil that he'd also taken cover. Better yet, Eli wanted Gunnar to be able to take out whoever was firing those shots. There was no chance this was just some random attack, and that meant either there was another hired gun or the boss was there to make sure the job was done right.

That sent a slam of rage through him. Here Ashlyn was in danger again, and they still didn't know why this was happening or who was behind it. That would change, though. As soon as he could get her safely out of here, Eli would make certain that he caught this SOB. First, however, he had to get Ashlyn out of here.

Eli's phone dinged with a text. Gunnar. Anyone hit? Do you have eyes on the shooter?

No to both, Eli texted back. He nearly added for Gunnar to make sure he stayed out of Eli's line of fire, but it wasn't necessary. Gunnar was a good cop and knew that Eli would be looking for this snake.

"Stay down," Eli told Ashlyn.

"You stay down, too," she insisted, her voice shaking.

No way could he do that. He couldn't give the shooter a chance to move closer to the house so he or she would have a kill shot.

Eli got up, took his backup weapon from his ankle holster and slid it her way. It would probably make her even more terrified than she already was, but the security system wasn't on, and that meant someone could sneak in. If that happened, he at least wanted her to have something to protect herself.

"Keep watch on the front door," he added. Again, that wasn't going to steady it, but Ashlyn was smart so she'd not only keep an eye out, she'd also listen for any sounds of footsteps.

"I have my phone now," Ashlyn said. "I'll text Kellan and tell him what's going on."

His brother would send backup, and it wouldn't take long for someone to get there. But Eli hoped he had this situation under control before a cruiser could respond. This time, though, maybe he'd be able to only injure the person so he could take them alive. And question them.

Two more shots came, but these didn't go crashing into the window. They hit the back door, a sign that the shooter was indeed moving. But Eli wouldn't stand still, either. He had to at least know the person's position to be able to stop them.

Staying down, he went to the window and peered out. He saw Gunnar by the barn—on the opposite side from where those shots had been fired. Good. That meant the deputy had some cover.

And could possibly be in a position to be ambushed.

Gunnar had his back against the barn wall, and with his gun gripped and ready, he was keeping watch. Still, that didn't mean someone couldn't take him out with a long-range shot.

Eli fired glances all around, but he didn't see their attacker. So he waited. Hard to do since this clown could send a deadly shot straight into the house. Still, he forced himself not to move and risk having the shooter see him.

Where the hell was he or she?

There was a fence, but Eli would be able to at least partially see him if he was there. That left some trees and shrubs just beyond the fence and a water trough just inside it, but Eli caught no glint of metal from a firearm, no movement.

Another shot came. It also hit the back door, but this one had a different angle, meaning the shooter had moved again. Since Eli still hadn't seen him or her that meant he or she was likely on the ground. A belly-down prone position wasn't the best if a gunman wanted to get off a series of rapid shots, but it was damn good for accuracy.

Eli tested that. He took off his hat and flung it at the window. Sure enough the shot came, and the bullet tore through it. Eli didn't need another reason to hate this piece of dirt, but that did it because it was his favorite hat. Still, it was worth the sacrifice because he now had this idiot's location.

The shooter was on the ground by a water trough.

Eli made a quick check on Ashlyn to make sure she was still down on the floor. She was. She had her phone in her left hand, the gun in her right, and her attention was fixed exactly where Eli needed it to be. On the front door.

With his back covered, Eli leaned out and sent a shot to the side of the trough where he'd pinpointed the gunman. His bullet only kicked up some dirt, but it was enough to get the guy scurrying to the side.

"He's by the trough," Eli called out to Gunnar. It was possible that Gunnar would have a better angle on the shot than he would.

From the corner of his eye, Eli watched the deputy lean out from cover. Eli did the same, and he waited for Gunnar to fire. Gunnar's shot slammed into the fence, sending a spray of splinters. Not a hit, but it got the gunman scrambling back toward the trees.

That's when Eli took his shot.

He sent a bullet right into the guy's shoulder, and Eli knew he'd hit pay dirt when the guy dropped to his knees. But he wasn't down. The idiot twisted his body, taking aim at Gunnar. And that's when Eli knew he had no choice.

He fired.

This time, it wasn't a shot to disable him but rather one that would likely kill. The shooter took two bullets to the side of his chest before he collapsed face-first onto the ground.

Chapter Ten

Ashlyn tried to make sure she looked a lot steadier than she felt. That's because Eli was watching her, no doubt to make sure she didn't fall apart.

She wouldn't.

No way did she want to add more to his shoulders than was already there.

Eli was blaming himself for the attack. She could sense that in his stiff posture and tight jaw as he paced across the living room and continued the string of calls that'd started as soon as he'd killed the gunman. Eli was angry and frustrated—two things that she completely understood. She had gone through that as well, but then it'd been eased some when she'd gotten back to Jack's and had seen for herself that Cora was okay. There hadn't been a second attack at the ranch.

She looked down at Cora, who was now in Ashlyn's lap, and the baby smiled around the bottle she was sucking. Ashlyn automatically smiled back and felt some more of the tension ease away. Things weren't perfect, not by a long shot, but it was impossible not to be at least somewhat happy with her baby cuddled like this in her arms.

Owen glanced over at her when Cora cooed, the sound obviously getting his attention. He wasn't pacing. He was in the kitchen with her, sipping coffee and standing guard. She didn't miss the quick checks he was making in the backyard. In the front room, Eli was doing the same in between his pacing.

Owen reached down, brushed his fingers over Cora's bare toes, causing the baby to smile again. "If you go back out with Eli when he questions the suspects, you'll leave her here with Raylene and me," Owen said.

It wasn't a question, but Ashlyn nodded anyway. She wouldn't take Cora out of the house, but the rest of what Owen said puzzled her.

"Is that what Eli's doing—setting up another round of interrogation?" she asked Owen.

He nodded, sipped his coffee and studied his brother. "I don't think his temper is going to help in the interviews."

No, it wouldn't. Eli had been forced to shoot two men who'd tried to kill them. Dealing with that alone was enough, but he had the added pressure of not knowing which of their suspects was behind this.

Remy, Dominick or Oscar.

All of them had means, motive and opportunity, which meant Eli and she weren't any closer to learning the truth than they had been before this latest attack. She knew that Eli hadn't had a choice about killing the gunman, but part of his anger and frustration had to be because now the man couldn't tell them who'd hired him.

"You might want to try to calm him down a little," Owen continued, tipping his head to Eli.

Ashlyn lifted her eyebrow. "Why would you think I could do that?"

"You always could," Owen assured her. "I remember at the end of a football game when someone on the opposing team gave him a sucker punch as they were heading to the locker rooms. Eli punched back, and likely would have kept on punching if you hadn't stopped it."

She had no trouble recalling that. Or the fact that it'd happened a decade and a half ago. "High school," she reminded him. "I don't have that kind of…influence over him now."

"Sure you do." Owen gave her a wink.

Ashlyn would have disagreed with that, but Owen didn't give her a chance. He scooped Cora up from her arms, kissing the baby on her cheek. Cora must have liked the move because she gave him a big smile.

"I'm good at burping detail," Owen insisted, and

he headed out of the kitchen just as Eli was coming in. Obviously, this was Owen's ploy to give her some privacy so she could try to do the soothing that he'd just suggested. She wouldn't.

Or rather she *couldn't.*

But it certainly seemed as if Eli needed something. As he got closer, she could practically feel the anger radiating off him.

"What the heck is he smiling about?" Eli growled when he looked in Owen's direction.

"Burping duty," Ashlyn mumbled, causing Eli to snap toward her. "He says he's good at it," she added when he just stared at her.

Skepticism replaced some of Eli's anger, and then his scowl deepened. "He told you to calm me down."

"Yes," she admitted. "I'd try if I thought it'd do any good." She took hold of his hand. "This wasn't your fault."

"The hell it wasn't. I knew it was a bad idea for you to go back to your place."

Ashlyn sighed. "All right, then it's my fault because I'm the one who insisted I go."

That didn't improve his glare. Not at first anyway. Then he groaned and squeezed his eyes shut a moment. When he opened them again, she'd hoped to see less anger there. Nope. So she leaned in and brushed her mouth over his. Eli stiffened, but when his gaze met hers, his eyes weren't nearly as narrowed as they had been.

Only then did she remember that she'd done that very thing the night of that football fight.

"You're trying to distract me," he grumbled. "But it'll take a hell of a lot more than just a kiss to do that."

Even though his tone was still rough, she relaxed a little because she could feel him doing the same. She wanted to push it even more. To say something light. But she still wasn't feeling steady enough to do that.

And Eli saw that in her eyes.

He cursed softly, pulled her to him and brushed a kiss on the top of her head. "You're going to have some bad dreams tonight," he whispered. "Not much I can do about that, so I'm sorry for that, too."

She pulled back, looked up at him. "I know there's plenty you will do to help with those dreams…and the threat of another attack." Things that involved more than hugs and kisses. "I heard one of your phone calls. You're bringing out some Ranger friends to search the grounds and keep watch. You're adding some security cameras with motion detectors. And I suspect you'll sleep on the hall floor outside the bedroom again."

He frowned. "How'd you know I slept in the hall?"

"Because I know you." Ashlyn ran a hand down

his arm and felt the muscles respond beneath her touch. "You'll do whatever it takes. So will I."

His frown had lightened up a little, but it deepened again when she added that last sentence. "What do you mean by that?"

Since this would require a deep breath, she took it. "Owen said you were bringing in all the suspects. When?"

"ASAP. I told them if they didn't get into the sheriff's office that I'd arrest them and charge them with obstruction of justice."

Ashlyn bet none of them cared much for that threat, but it might get them there sooner than later. "I think that's a good idea, but I also believe I should be there when you talk to them."

Now his eyes narrowed, too.

"We won't take Cora with us," she went on. "She'll stay here with an army of law enforcement officers to protect her. She'll be safe." Ashlyn had to believe that because the alternative was unthinkable. "But I should be there to talk to Dominick. I know him. I've dealt with him. And if he's lying, I believe I'd be able to tell."

Eli didn't jump to respond to that. Not verbally, anyway. However, he did grind out some profanity under his breath. "It might not even be Dominick. It could be Remy. Hell, or Oscar. I'm trying to get an ID on this latest shooter so I can see if he's linked to Oscar like the others."

She nodded. Ashlyn had heard bits of that conversation as well. "And if he is, maybe you'll have enough to make an arrest."

"Yeah." Eli didn't sound very hopeful about that, though. "I also asked the Rangers to do a deeper financial dig on Dominick and Remy."

Good. She hadn't heard that part of the call, but Dominick was definitely capable of hiding funds. She suspected Remy was, too, especially if he'd hired someone to murder the mortician and steal those files.

"It just seems stupid that Oscar would hire gunmen that we could so easily connect back to him," Eli continued. He paused, groaned softly. "But then that might have been exactly why Oscar would do that."

A sort of reverse psychology, she supposed, but it might not be as complicated as that. It could be that Oscar was reacting out of anger and hired the first people he could think of. Even as the owner of a seedy pawnshop, there probably wasn't a slew of potential candidates for hit men so he might not have had a lot of options in that area.

"The timeline bothers me," Eli went on. "I mean, Oscar waiting so long to come after us. It makes me wonder if he's working with one of the other suspects."

Interesting. Ashlyn hadn't considered that, but it was possible either with Remy or Dominick. One of them could have stirred up Oscar's old anger enough to cause the man to snap.

"If that's true, maybe both of them paid the gunmen," she threw out there. "If so, there would be smaller amounts withdrawn from their individual accounts." Which wouldn't be good because it would make those payments harder to find.

Eli nodded and absently ran his hand down her back. "Remy must have known that he'd be a suspect right from the get-go, so I'm betting he would have made sure a suspicious withdrawal didn't show up in his account."

Ashlyn made a sound of agreement. "It's the same for Dominick."

He nodded again, paused. "But if we go with the theory of two of them working together, Remy or Oscar could have given Dominick the names of the gunmen. Those men might have connections to Remy, too."

Eli's phone rang, the sound jangling her nerves more than it should have. Any unexpected noise was having that effect on her, which meant Eli was right, too, about this latest attack giving her another round of bad dreams.

"It's Gus," Eli said when he looked at his phone screen, and as he'd done with some of the other calls, he put it on speaker.

Ashlyn checked the clock on the stove. There'd been enough time for the exhumation, so Gus was likely calling about that. She stepped back a little and tried to tamp down the nerves that were already firing beneath the surface of her skin. She also tried to brace herself for whatever Gus was about to tell them.

Gus made a hoarse sob, and with just that sound alone, Ashlyn heard the heavy emotion. "She's not there," Gus blurted out, his voice choppy. "Marta's not there in the grave. The coffin is empty."

ELI FELT AS if someone had slugged him in the gut. Hell. What was going on?

"This means my girl is alive," Gus continued a moment later. "Alive," he repeated, crying now. "I have to find her."

Eli agreed with that, but it didn't answer a really big question. How had Marta managed to pull this off? Eli could figure out the why. Well, if he was to believe Oscar. Marta had faked her death to hide from some drug lords with ties to Drake.

But that didn't feel right.

"I'm going to make some calls," Gus went on. "The first will be to Remy—"

"Hold off on doing that. Remy should be arriving at the sheriff's office here in Longview Ridge at any moment," Eli explained. "I want to see how he reacts when I tell him Marta's body wasn't in the coffin."

"Remy will know where she is," Gus argued. "I need to talk to him."

"If you tip him off, Remy might go rabbit on us. He's got the money to do that now, and if he disappears, we might lose our best chance at finding out where Marta is. Just hold off talking to him for a couple of hours—that's all I'm asking."

"My daughter's alive." The man's voice broke. Then he paused. "I'll give you those two hours, but I'm coming to talk to Remy in person."

Eli knew he stood no chance of talking Gus out of doing that. If their positions had been reversed, no one could have convinced Eli to stay back while the law got involved. That's why he just thanked Gus and ended the call.

"Let me make a quick check on Cora, and I'll go with you to Kellan's office," Ashlyn insisted.

He wasn't surprised she was sticking to her guns on this. Especially now. Marta had been her best friend, and if the woman was truly alive, then Remy would almost certainly know where she was.

"Am I staying here or going with you?" Gunnar asked Eli after Ashlyn hurried into the bedroom.

"You're coming with us. I can't guarantee you, though, that you won't get shot at again."

Gunnar lifted his shoulder. "I'm hoping we've met our bullet quota for the day. Plus, Owen and Raylene are better with baby-guarding duty than I am."

Eli could agree with all of that. Or rather he wanted to agree on the bullet quota, but there could be another hired gun. While he waited at the front door, he wondered if it would do any good to remind Ashlyn of that. It wouldn't, he decided. She was seeing the big picture here, and that meant they had to cut off the head of this snake to stop any other attacks.

He made a quick call to Kellan to update him about Marta and asked his brother to pass along the info to SAPD. Since the cops there were primary on the mortician's murder, they'd want to know. And they would almost certainly want their own interview with Remy.

"Be careful," Owen warned Gunnar and Eli as he came out of the bedroom with Ashlyn. "Don't worry. We'll keep watch," he added to Ashlyn. "And there are two Rangers on the grounds along with the hands. We'll make sure no one gets to Cora."

She thanked him, and as if it were the most natural thing in the world, she gave Owen a quick hug. It was amazing how an intense life-threatening situation could change things. It was as if they'd stepped back in time to when she'd cared for Owen like a brother.

And Eli as a lover.

It riled him that his mind kept going back to that. He had plenty of things to do, and none of them involved taking Ashlyn to bed.

Even before they hurried out to the cruiser, Eli glanced out the window, looking for any kind of threat. Both Gunnar and Ashlyn did the same, but Eli didn't see anything other than some armed ranch hands who were clearly standing guard.

"Remy might have murdered the mortician," Ashlyn said as she, too, kept watch.

Eli made a sound of agreement. That was one of the first things that had occurred to him, and he'd need to press Remy on not only his alibi but that deeper search into his financials. Motive was easy to figure out. Remy wanted to keep it secret that Marta was alive. But that only worked if Remy was aware of that. He might not be.

"Thanks for not giving me an argument about this," Ashlyn murmured a moment later, drawing his attention back to her.

Eli hoped he didn't regret giving in on this, but he had to consider that whoever had hired those gunmen would be getting desperate. Three hired killers—all dead. That was a lot of money down the drain, and that had to be beyond frustrating for the person who'd hired them.

His phone dinged with a text, and Eli read the info that Kellan had just sent him. And he cursed. "They got an ID on the latest dead gunman. Jay Hamby. I know him. He was a criminal informant."

Ashlyn shifted in the seat toward him. "I never heard Marta mention him." But then she shook her head. "She didn't talk about that side of her life very often, though. Is Hamby connected to Oscar, too?"

"Don't know yet, but that's something I intend to find out." However, Eli was guessing that would be a yes, that there was indeed a connection. Now he'd need to figure out if Hamby had been hired to frame Oscar or if Oscar had just tapped someone that he already knew to do the job.

"How soon do you have Oscar and Dominick coming into the sheriff's office?" she asked.

"They might already be there. I didn't exactly treat them with kid gloves when I ordered them to come in."

That, of course, meant they'd be showing up with their lawyers. Eli didn't mind that. He just wanted them in the box so he could grill them about both of the attacks.

The moment that Gunnar pulled to a stop in front of the sheriff's office, Eli spotted Remy, who appeared to be pacing across the reception area. He looked about as riled as Eli was. Ditto for the suit—the lawyer, no doubt. He was a wiry man with white hair and a steely expression. Eli gave him steel right back, and he knew for a fact that he was better at it.

"What the hell is this about now?" Remy snapped the moment they were all inside.

Eli didn't answer but instead turned to Kellan, who was sipping coffee while standing in the bullpen. "I frisked Remy. He's not armed. And I read him his rights."

That was exactly how Eli wanted to start this meeting. "This way," he told Remy.

Eli started toward the interview room. That would not only get this started, it would also take Ashlyn away from the windows. Eli was about to tell her that she'd have to wait in observation for this leg of the chat, but Remy started up before they even reached the room.

"I asked you a question," Remy went on, his voice as sharp as a bullwhip. "Why did you say you'd arrest me if I didn't come in? I've cooperated with you, and I've done nothing wrong." Remy opened his mouth again, no doubt to continue his verbal fire, but Eli stopped him cold.

"Marta's coffin is empty," Eli said, turning in the hall so he could study every bit of Remy's reaction. By telling him this way, Ashlyn would be able to do the same. "There's no body."

Remy pulled back his shoulders, his gaze firing to Ashlyn as if he expected her to confirm or deny that. She didn't say a word. Neither did Eli. They both just stood there, waiting.

"No body," Remy repeated. Groaning, he spun around, pressing his head to the wall. Eli was skeptical enough to believe the man had done that to hide his expression rather than his attempt to deal with the shock.

"What's this about?" the lawyer asked. "What's going on?"

But Remy waved him off. With his breath coming out in short bursts, Remy finally turned back around to face him. "How'd you find this out?"

"Marta's father had the body exhumed," Eli answered, still watching Remy. There wasn't so much shock or surprise now, but something else. Urgency, maybe?

"Where's Marta?" Remy demanded. "Did Gus say?"

The tone seemed right for a man who'd just been given a big shock like this, but Eli wasn't ready to buy it just yet. "Gus doesn't know. Do you? Do you know where she is?"

"Of course not." The anger flared through Remy's eyes again. "I had no idea. I went to her funeral. I watched them put her coffin in the ground."

Eli didn't point out that a burial could be faked as well as a death. Instead, he went with another facet of this. "Did you steal Marta's hospital and funeral home records?" he came out and asked.

"No," Remy howled while the lawyer barked out a protest about Eli badgering his client. The noise must have alerted Kellan because he stepped into the hall with them.

"A problem?" Kellan calmly said.

"Yes!" Remy snapped. "Your brother just accused me of murder."

Eli lifted his shoulder. "I hadn't gotten around to doing that, not specifically, but the question would have come up soon enough. A missing body and files. A dead mortician. And you with a recent inheritance. That could all equal a whole lot of felonies."

That set the lawyer off howling again, and Kellan merely tipped his head to the interview room. "Why don't I start this interrogation with Remy? There's something on my desk that I think you need to see."

Part of Eli wanted to stay put and yank the information from Remy, but judging from Kellan's expression, whatever was on his desk was important.

Eli put his hand on Ashlyn's back to get her moving out of the hall. They didn't get far, though. That's because Oscar came in.

"I don't appreciate being ordered in here like this," Oscar grumbled.

"Welcome to the club." Eli tipped his head to Remy. "Others feel the same as you."

Oscar looked at Remy just as Remy turned in his direction. Their gazes practically collided. "I know you," Remy spat out.

Oscar's eyes narrowed. "So? A lot of people know me."

"You were friends with Drake." Remy's eyes had narrowed, too. "You're the one who helped Leon set up the attack in that alley."

Eli hadn't counted on being the one who was

surprised today, but that did it. "How'd you know Oscar and Drake were friends?" Eli asked Remy.

Remy's shoulders snapped back again, just as they'd done when Eli had told him about Marta's empty coffin. But this time it wasn't shock, pretend or otherwise. Eli was pretty sure this was raw anger.

"How did you know Oscar and Drake were friends?" Eli repeated when Remy didn't answer.

"I need to talk with my client," the lawyer insisted, taking Remy by the arm. Remy didn't put up a protest when the attorney led him into the interview room.

Since this delay might give Remy plenty of time to doctor his answer, Eli turned to Oscar. "You know Remy?"

Oscar didn't dodge the question. "I know of him. He was Marta's hotheaded boyfriend. I'm guessing he's got some kind of grudge against me. Like you," he added to Eli.

"No grudge," Eli assured him. "Just looking for the truth."

Kellan took things from there. "Come this way to interview room two, and we can get started. No lawyer?"

"He's on the way," Oscar said, but his attention wasn't on them. It was on the room where Remy's attorney had taken him.

Later, Eli would want to know if Oscar was the one who was holding grudges and if the man knew anything about Marta's whereabouts. For now, though, Eli sent off a text to one of his Ranger friends to request a favor, and then he went with Ashlyn to Kellan's office. It didn't take him long to see the report that his brother had left for him on the center of his desk.

"It's the detailed financials on Dominick that the Rangers ran," Eli relayed to her as he scanned through it. It didn't take him long to see what had caught Kellan's eye.

A second bank account that had been hidden under several layers of security.

Ashlyn made a strangled sound of surprise because she'd seen it, too. And the info just below that.

Dominick obviously had some explaining to do.

Chapter Eleven

Twenty-five thousand dollars.

That was a lot of money, and Ashlyn immediately thought of how Dominick could have used it—to hire those three gunmen.

"Yeah," Eli grumbled, letting her know they were having the same train of thought. "He's got means, motive and opportunity."

Dominick did, but it sickened her to even consider that he'd want her dead so he would stand a better chance of getting custody of Cora. And that sent a new wave of alarm through her.

"Olive Landry. Cora's biological mother," she managed to say. "She could be in danger."

Eli nodded so quickly that it meant he'd already considered it. "I alerted Austin PD to the possibility of that. They've been checking on her. I'll have them talk to her to see if she wants police protection."

Ashlyn didn't exactly breathe easier about that,

but she was glad Eli was already on top of it. Maybe it would be enough. While she was hoping, she added that maybe Oscar and Remy would give them some information that would help put an end to the danger.

"Dominick should be here soon," Eli reminded her. "But I'd like to hear what Remy's saying to Kellan."

Ashlyn did as well, and she followed Eli to observation, which was located between the two interview rooms. Oscar sat alone in one of them, but Kellan appeared to already be deep into questioning Remy. Remy looked just as flustered and upset as he had been earlier when he'd confronted Oscar.

"You believe Remy didn't know about Marta's empty grave?" Ashlyn came out and asked.

"I'm not sure. He's lying about something. What, exactly, I don't know. But if Marta's truly alive, I can't see Remy not knowing about it."

She agreed, so maybe what Remy was lying about was his part in the attacks. After all, he had money, too, and while there had been a cash withdrawal from his account, it wasn't as large as the one Dominick had made. However, it didn't mean Remy hadn't gotten his hands on the cash to do the job.

"If Oscar knew the gunmen, Remy could have, too," Eli pointed out. Then he paused. "But without the money trail, we don't have probable cause to hold Remy. Besides, letting him go might give us more answers."

Ashlyn looked at him and thought about that for a moment. "You're going to put a tail on him?"

Eli nodded. "If he knows anything about Marta, we'll soon find out."

Good. Even if Remy wasn't up to something illegal, they might be able to exclude him as a suspect. And if he was guilty, then Eli could arrest him. However, this could go well beyond that.

If Marta was alive, Remy might lead them to her.

Just considering that possibility sent Ashlyn's heart into a tailspin. All this time she'd grieved for her friend. No, more than that. She'd felt guilty for not being able to save Marta. Ashlyn would be relieved if Marta was actually alive, but it was going to cause an avalanche of emotions that her friend had let her believe that she was dead. And more. Maybe Marta had been the one to hire the gunmen.

Ashlyn continued to watch as Kellan pressed Remy on the subject of those hired guns. And as expected, Remy denied everything. No way would he just confess to hiring hit men when there was no solid evidence against him. Kellan pressed on Marta, too, but again nothing. After that, Kellan was forced to let him go.

Remy stormed out, and as he went past the observation room, he shot Eli and her a glare. Kellan came out as well. No glare from him. Just the same signs of frustration that Ashlyn was sure were on her face.

"I need some coffee," Kellan said to Eli. "If you've got anything to ask Oscar, you'd better do it now before I start the official interview."

Ashlyn knew that was the advantage of having a brother who was a sheriff. If Kellan had gone by the book on this, Eli and she wouldn't have been a part of this.

Eli thanked Kellan and didn't waste any time going into the interview room with Oscar. Ashlyn stayed right by Eli's side in the doorway.

"You're here to have another go at me," Oscar immediately snarled.

"Jay Hamby," Eli said, not responding to the man's comment.

As Ashlyn had done with Remy, she watched Oscar to see how he reacted to that name. But Oscar merely shrugged. "I know him. He's a bouncer at a bar just up the street from my shop."

Eli didn't say anything else. He just stared at Oscar and waited for the man to continue.

Oscar finally cursed, and his mouth twisted as if he'd gotten a bad taste of something. "Let me guess—he's the guy you shot and killed at Ashlyn's place."

"How'd you know about that?" Eli fired back.

"Word gets around." Oscar cursed again, shook his head. "And now I get why I'm here. You think because I know...*knew* Jay Hamby that I hired him to take shots at you. I didn't."

"Any reason I should believe you?" Eli asked.

Oscar's eyes narrowed to slits. "Yeah. Because it's the truth." He looked away from Eli and repeated some of that profanity he'd been spewing. "Someone's trying to set me up. That's the only explanation as to why all three hired guns could be connected back to me."

"Not the only explanation," Eli assured him. "You could be guilty. Are you?"

Oscar's gaze came back to Eli. "No. And I'm not saying another word until my lawyer gets here."

Eli made a suit-yourself sound and walked away, leading Ashlyn back in the direction of Kellan's office. Kellan was on the phone, and he held up his finger for them to wait a second while he finished. Ashlyn tuned in to the conversation when she heard Kellan say, "Ashlyn's horses."

She certainly hadn't forgotten about her horses or her small ranch, but it was a reminder that one of the animals could have been hurt. After Eli had shot the gunman, he'd gotten her out of there so fast that she hadn't had time to check for herself.

"Everything's okay," Kellan assured her as soon as he finished the call. "The CSIs are out at your place again, and I sent two of my ranch hands out to tend your livestock and get your things."

"Thank you." She hadn't realized just how thin

her breath had gotten until she tried to speak. "I'd already packed a suitcase, but I left it on the floor in the kitchen."

He nodded and sent a text. No doubt to let his hands know where it was. "I've also arranged for Cora's crib to be taken to Jack's." Kellan scrubbed his hand over his face. "I considered moving all of you back to Eli's since it's bigger, but I think it's safer if she stays put."

Ashlyn felt the same way, but there was something in Kellan's weary eyes that made her realize there was more.

"The CSIs found Hamby's car," Kellan added several moments later. "It was parked on a side road just up from Ashlyn's. There are signs that two people were in the vehicle. Two fast-food bags and drinks. Hamby also had a burner cell phone in it, and he got a call right after he was shot. It came from another burner."

Ashlyn followed the thread of that. "There's a fourth gunman?"

"Probably," Kellan admitted. "Either that or the person who hired him could have been in the vehicle. If so, that rules out Remy, because he has an alibi. He said he was at a doctor's appointment, and I just confirmed that."

"Any prints or trace in Hamby's car?" Eli asked.

"Plenty. Along with the receipt for the fast food.

It'll take them a while to sort through all of it, but we might get lucky."

Maybe, but she wondered if whoever had hired Hamby would be careless enough to leave evidence behind.

Kellan tipped his head to the man in the suit who came in the front door. "Oscar's lawyer. I'll get started with the interview, and when I'm done, I'll press the CSIs to get us anything they can from that car." He started out but then stopped, his gaze connecting with Eli's. "Dominick should be in soon. You want to interview him?"

"Absolutely. I want to ask him about his secret bank account and that big withdrawal."

Ashlyn knew it would take more luck to pin Dominick down on that. Especially if he had indeed hired those gunmen.

As soon as Kellan walked out, Eli took hold of her hand and moved her out of the doorway. Out of view from the windows, too. She hadn't needed a reminder of the danger, but that gave her one anyway.

"There are too many puzzle pieces," she said. "In the meantime, you and I—maybe Cora, too— are in the crosshairs of a killer."

He didn't argue with her. Couldn't. Because it was true, a frustration that they both felt. That frustration was in every muscle of his body when he pulled her into his arms. As he'd done in the kitchen, he brushed a kiss on the top of her head. A kiss of comfort.

And it worked.

Ashlyn could practically feel some of the tension slide right out of her. Of course, the heat came in its place. No surprise there. She'd been dealing with it for much too long.

He pulled back just a little and looked down at her with those smoky gray eyes. They weren't stormy now but had some of the same fire that she was certain was in her own.

"Yeah," he said as if he'd known exactly what she was thinking—and feeling. "If we were still in high school, I would just coax you into taking a trip out to my truck. That won't work this time, though."

"No." Since he could be dangerous. And also since sex should be the last thing on their minds. But Ashlyn wanted to make this moment a little lighter than spelling out those reminders. "Because we're sensible adults now."

The corner of his mouth lifted, causing a dimple to flash in his cheek. Yes, a dimple. It was another weapon in the arsenal of Eli Slater, hot cowboy. But the smile didn't last long.

"Soon, we're going to have a brief talk about this," Eli drawled, his voice all smoke and heat. "And then we'll deal with it. I've got some ideas as to how we can do that."

Now she smiled, and even though she figured

it was a mistake, Ashlyn brushed her mouth over his. Again, not a full-fledged kiss, but it could have qualified as foreplay. *Short* foreplay. They moved away from each other when they heard a familiar voice in the squad room.

Dominick.

Ashlyn whirled around, and the first thing she noticed was that Dominick had seen her in Eli's arms. She silently groaned. She didn't especially want to keep her feelings for Eli secret, but she figured it wasn't going to please Dominick. Of course, nothing would likely please him at this point.

"I see you've found a way to keep yourself busy," Dominick snapped. "And where's Cora while you're here with Slater?"

"Cora's safe," Ashlyn settled for saying.

With his lawyer right on his heels, Dominick came closer. "I want to see her, to make sure you're not lying to me."

"Uh, you're here for an official interrogation," Eli interrupted. "Not to visit a baby. So you can just cut the demands. The only rights you have are to remain silent and have your attorney present. That's it."

Dominick's icy gaze cut to Eli. "I'm here because Ashlyn has talked you into harassing me. What the hell do you want this time?"

Eli stepped out and used his fingers to motion for Dominick to follow him, but Eli made sure that he was between Dominick and her. On the way to the interview, he recited Dominick his rights. That only added more steel and ice to Dominick's expression.

"You'll have to wait in the observation room," Eli whispered to her. "I need to keep this official."

She nodded, though she would have preferred to confront Dominick face-to-face. Still, she'd be able to see him and gauge his reaction. It was obvious he was more upset now than he had been during his other visit.

So was she, Ashlyn realized.

Dominick's demand to see Cora had cut her to the bone. And also riled her. If he truly was so interested in the baby's safety, then why would he insist on seeing her at a time like this? She'd already known Dominick was pigheaded and used to getting his way, but he had also claimed to love Cora. If that was true, he sure wasn't putting his granddaughter first.

Ashlyn flipped the switch to get the audio, and she listened while Eli worked his way through some preliminary questions. Dominick didn't hesitate when questioned about his alibi during the time of the latest attack. He said he was in a meeting with four other people. She didn't doubt it, either. If he was behind this, then he would have made sure of a strong alibi.

"Tell me about your secret bank account," Eli

threw out there the moment Dominick had answered the previous question.

Dominick visibly stiffened, opened his mouth. Probably to claim there was no such account. But then he stopped and had a short whispered conversation with his lawyer.

"It's not a secret," Dominick said when he faced Eli again. "It's an account I'd set up so I'd have funds to buy my wife gifts and such. That way, whatever I bought her would be a surprise. After she died, I didn't close it. Sentimental reasons," he added with a smirk.

"Sentimental reasons," Eli repeated. No smirk, but he sounded plenty skeptical. "The account had a lot of layers of security on it for something that's supposed to be legal and aboveboard."

Dominick calmly lifted his shoulder. "My late wife was very good at snooping."

"Yeah." Eli's skepticism went up a notch, but Ashlyn knew that with the woman dead it wasn't something they could prove. "Do you use the account for things other than surprise gifts?"

Now a faint smile crossed Dominick's lips. "Yes. Recently, I withdrew funds to do some remodeling at my house."

"Really?" Eli challenged. "You used cash for that?"

"Yes. I thought it'd make things easier for the

contractor. And before you ask, there was nothing illegal about it."

"You've got receipts?" Eli pressed.

"I can get them." Dominick no longer smiled or looked smug. The anger was creeping back into his expression and tone.

While Eli continued to press him on that, Ashlyn took out her phone and called Sue Malloy, the nanny Dominick had hired for his visits with Cora. Even though Ashlyn had never left Cora with the woman, Sue had given Ashlyn her number.

"Ashlyn," Sue said the moment she answered. "I was surprised when I saw your name on my phone screen. I heard about the attack. Are Cora and you okay?"

"Yes. We're fine. But that's not why I'm calling." She paused, tried to figure out how to say this. She didn't want to put the woman on defensive. "Have you recently been at Dominick's house?"

"I have," she readily admitted. "He converted one of the bedrooms to a nursery. You know, in case he got the overnight visits approved for Cora. He wanted her to have her own room, and he asked me to make sure it had everything she might need."

Considering that Dominick was a suspect in attempted murders, that tightened Ashlyn's stomach, but she reminded herself that he could be innocent. He hadn't lied about the bank account, and while it still didn't seem aboveboard, he had told the truth about the renovation.

"Is there a problem?" Sue asked.

"No. I was just checking. Thanks." And she ended the call before Sue could press her for more info.

This time when Ashlyn looked at Dominick through the glass, she did so with less anger and nerves. Maybe he was innocent about everything other than wanting more time with his granddaughter. If so, she'd owe him an apology, but she wasn't about to do that until the person who'd hired those gunmen had been caught.

She heard the footsteps in the hall and automatically tensed again. But it wasn't a threat that her body was preparing for. It was Gunnar. He glanced through both observation windows. Kellan was still in interview with Oscar. Eli with Dominick.

"Any idea how close they are to wrapping things up?" Gunnar asked.

"It shouldn't be long on Dominick. I'm not sure about Oscar." She hadn't been listening to that interrogation.

"Good. Because Eli's going to want to hear this." Gunnar went to the interview room door and knocked. "The tail we had on Remy just called, and he says something suspicious is going on and that Eli should get out there right away."

Chapter Twelve

Eli took one look at Ashlyn and Gunnar, and he knew something was wrong. Something that was going to delay finishing his interview with Dominick. He stepped out into the hall with them, shutting the door in case this was news about that hidden bank account.

"The reserve deputy, Manuel Garcia, we had on Remy followed him to a small farmhouse about ten miles from here," Gunnar explained. He glanced down and read from a note he was holding. "The place belonged to Remy's grandmother. It's in his name now, but it's been empty for a couple of years since the grandmother got moved into a nursing home."

Eli took a moment to process that but figured there had to be more or Gunnar wouldn't have pulled him out of the interview. "What happened?"

"Garcia parked on a trail so he could keep watch, and he saw Remy go to the backyard. He says that

Remy then dropped down and started crying in front of what Garcia thinks is maybe a headstone. You know, a grave."

Beside him, Ashlyn made a sharp sound of surprise. "Are any of his relatives buried there?" she asked.

Gunnar shook his head. "There's no burial record for anyone at that location, and Garcia figured the way that Remy was carrying on that it probably wasn't a pet." Gunnar paused. "I thought you'd want us to go there and check things out."

"I do." Eli had to give the logistics of that some thought. "Get the cruiser ready, and I'll let Kellan know what's going on."

Eli was about to tell Ashlyn that she'd be staying there at the sheriff's office, but then he considered that she would be there with two of their prime suspects. Of course, Kellan would protect her, but his brother already had his hands full with the interviews.

"You want to come with Gunnar and me?" Eli asked her.

She gave each of the interview doors a glimpse and then nodded.

Eli hoped like the devil that it wasn't another mistake, but this could be a "damned if he did, damned if he didn't" situation. Rather than stand there and lose time, he went in and had a quick chat with Kellan. Once he got the green light from his brother to leave, Eli headed toward the front.

Gunnar and Ashlyn were already there, waiting for him, and they rushed out and into the cruiser. Gunnar took off as they all kept watch around them. However, keeping watch wouldn't be easy with this trip because it was already starting to get dark.

Great.

Just what he didn't want—more obstacles to keeping Ashlyn safe.

"A grave," Ashlyn said. She still sounded shocked about that. "Maybe it's some kind of memorial for Marta?"

Yeah, that had been his first thought, shortly followed by the possibility that it could be a ploy to throw them off the scent that Marta might be alive. If Remy showed them a memorial like that, he might believe it would convince them to stop looking for the woman.

It wouldn't.

But maybe Remy was desperate.

Eli heard Gunnar's phone ding with a text, and the deputy passed it back to Eli so he could read it. What he saw on the screen had Eli cursing.

"Garcia says that Remy's walking away from the headstone," Eli relayed to Gunnar and Ashlyn before he handed it back to Gunnar. "It looks as if Remy is about to leave."

Eli wanted Remy on scene, and there was little

chance they would make it there in time before he left, so Eli took out his own phone. He didn't have Remy's number in his cell so he went through dispatch to have them call the man. Eli wasn't sure Remy would even answer, but he did on the fourth ring.

"Who the hell is this?" Remy snapped.

"Eli Slater. Just checking to see how you are." Eli didn't bother to sound sincere since Remy wouldn't have believed him anyway.

"How the hell do you think I am?" Remy countered, and Eli had no trouble hearing the man's sob.

"Did something happen?" Eli pressed. "Are you okay?"

Remy didn't jump to answer that time, and then he cursed much as Eli had done just seconds earlier. "I see a car. You had someone follow me." It wasn't a question. "You SOB. You put a tail on me."

"Yeah, I did," Eli readily admitted. "Now, you want to explain to me who's buried in that grave you were just crying over?"

That only brought on more cursing, and Eli waited him out while he mouthed for Ashlyn to use Gunnar's phone to keep track of Remy through Garcia. If Remy tried to leave, he wanted Garcia to stop him.

"You had no right to follow me," Remy finally said.

"I beg to differ. The badge gives me that right.

Now tell me who's in the grave, or I'll get a bull-dozer out there tonight, and I'll have it dug up."

"You can't!" Remy shouted. He repeated that a couple more times and broke down into another sob.

Ashlyn nudged Eli to show him Garcia's text message. Remy's pacing in the backyard. He's not heading back toward his car.

Good. He wanted Garcia to have backup before he tried to restrain Remy. The man could be armed. Heck, and he could be dangerous.

"I won't let you dig it up," Remy insisted.

"Then tell me who's buried there." Of course, Eli would have it dug up anyway, no matter what Remy told him.

Remy sobbed several more seconds, which Eli considered a good thing. Each second brought them closer to the place.

"She's here," Remy finally said on a choked breath. "Marta's here."

Eli felt the stillness slide through him. "Marta's buried in that grave?"

Again, Remy paused, cried. "Yes. She's here. I couldn't have her buried so far away. I needed to be able to come and talk to her. I needed her to be close to me."

The stillness didn't last inside Eli. A new wave of grief came, and it was just as raw and fresh as it had been the night Marta had been gunned down.

For a few hours, he'd allowed some part of himself to believe that she might be alive. But she wasn't.

"How'd you get Marta's body?" Eli pressed.

"The mortician," Remy answered after a long pause. "I bribed him, but I didn't kill him. I swear, I didn't."

Eli wasn't going to take the man's word for that. "And what about Marta's hospital records?"

"I didn't take those. There would have been no use in me doing that because she was dead. I only wanted her body so she could be close to me."

Eli tried to think of a reason why Remy wouldn't admit to stealing records when he'd just confessed to much worse, but he couldn't come up with anything. Well, unless Remy was just so upset that he had no idea what he was saying.

Ashlyn nudged Eli's arm again and showed him Garcia's latest text. Remy's walking toward a small barn that's off the backyard. You think he's in danger from himself?

Eli had to shrug. He had no idea what was going on in Remy's mind right now. "Tell Garcia to keep watching," he mouthed. "When I get there, we'll go inside the barn and arrest Remy."

And that would be just the start.

He'd need to do a tough interrogation with Remy and put in a call to Gus to let him know what was going on. Oh, and arrange for the body to be exhumed. Judging from Remy's extreme reaction and his confession, Eli figured this time they would indeed find Marta.

"Remy?" Eli asked.

No answer. And a moment later, Remy ended the call.

"We're almost there," Gunnar whispered as he took a turn off the main road. "We're only a couple of minutes out."

Good, because if Remy truly was suicidal, they needed to stop him. Maybe they would get there in time.

Gunnar's phone rang. Not a text this time, but a call from Garcia. Eli took the cell from Ashlyn and put the call on speaker.

"We've got a problem," Garcia immediately said. "Some guy just came out from the trees that aren't too far from the barn. He's got a gun."

Hell.

Eli had no trouble hearing what Garcia had said, and he felt the immediate slash of fresh adrenaline. Not again. Not another attack.

"Gunnar, turn off your headlights," Eli instructed. "When you reach Garcia's car, pull in behind him."

Eli looked ahead and spotted the unmarked sedan, and Gunnar came to a stop behind it. He saw the deputy crouched behind his door, and he had night goggles pressed to his eyes. The house and barn were in the distance, not far at all, but there were no signs of Remy or a gunman.

"I'm sorry," Eli said to Ashlyn, causing her to look at him. "We have to stay. We have to give Garcia backup."

"Of course you do." She kept her shoulders straight, trying to show him that she was a lot stronger than she likely felt. "I know the drill. I'll stay in the cruiser and will keep down."

It wasn't enough. Nowhere near it. But maybe this "damned if you do, damned if you don't" situation would end without Ashlyn getting hurt.

"Stay here with Ashlyn and call for backup," Eli told Gunnar, and Eli brushed a quick kiss on her mouth before he reached for the door.

"Be careful." Her voice was shaky now, and even in the dim light he saw the fear in her eyes.

"I will be," he promised her as he hurried out.

He eased the door shut so that it wouldn't make any noise, and he heard the clicks of Gunnar locking it. Eli trusted the deputy and knew he'd do whatever it took to keep Ashlyn safe, but Eli hated that he couldn't be in two places at once.

"The guy with the gun is on the left side of the barn," Garcia told him when Eli reached him, and he passed his goggles to Eli.

Eli didn't have any trouble spotting the man. Tall, lanky, dressed all in black. And he did indeed have a gun.

"Remy's still in the barn," Garcia added.

He hoped Remy wasn't doing something dangerous in there, but for now Eli had to go with the immediate threat—the gunman. The guy wasn't moving, but that didn't mean he soon wouldn't be. But who was his target?

Remy?

Or had the gunman known that Remy would lead them here?

"I'm going to cut around on foot and try to come up behind the thug," Eli instructed Garcia. "You move closer to the barn—also on foot—but try to keep an eye on the cruiser. I don't want them getting ambushed."

Garcia made a sound of agreement, and keeping low, the deputy started moving—fast. Eli did the same, after he put his phone on vibrate, and he tried to push aside any thoughts of all the things that could go wrong. So far, all the breaks had gone against them, and something had to go their way.

Despite it being past sunset, it was still hot, and it didn't take long for the sweat to start trickling down Eli's back. He swiped his forehead with the back of his hand and kept going. Kept listening. And watching. There was still no sign of Remy, but once Eli reached the house, he got a better look at the gunman. His attention was fastened to the barn.

And that's where he had his weapon aimed.

So, he was after Remy. Well, maybe. Since the

guy hadn't fired a shot, it could be that this was a setup to make them believe that Remy was a target.

As Eli got closer, he tamped down the thud of his heart so that it wouldn't interfere with his hearing, and took extra care to make sure his footsteps stayed light. He definitely didn't want to do anything to alert this clown.

He threaded his way through the trees, cursing when the underbrush crunched beneath his boots. The gunman immediately whipped in the direction of the sound—just as Eli managed to duck out of sight.

Eli stayed still, but thankfully he didn't hear the gunman coming his way. When he peeked out, he saw that the guy's focus was back on the barn.

Blowing out a quick breath of relief, Eli started moving again, and he made sure he maneuvered himself behind the man. That's when he realized the guy didn't have his weapon actually pointed at the barn. He was just watching.

Why?

Had someone sent him here to keep an eye on Remy, or was this going to be another attempted murder? Eli hoped he got the chance to find out.

He stopped just long enough to glance across the yard to see if he could spot Garcia. No sign of him, which was a good thing. It meant the deputy was managing to stay hidden enough while he made his way to the barn.

Soon, very soon, backup would be arriving, and they would make a silent approach. Maybe it wouldn't catch the attention of the gunman, because Eli didn't want the guy even looking in Ashlyn's direction. He wanted her safe, and the best way to do that was to stop this potential threat.

Eli crept closer, thankful for a gust of wind that muffled his move. Thankful, too, when the gunman's next glance was in the wrong direction. Eli was on his blind side, and he took full advantage of that.

"I'm Sergeant Eli Slater, Texas Ranger. Drop that gun or you're a dead man," Eli warned him.

The gunman spun around, getting ready to take aim, but Eli already had him beat. His weapon was ready to blast the snake to smithereens. Plus, Eli was still partly behind cover of one of the trees.

The man froze. Cursed. And Eli saw the exact moment the guy realized he was outgunned and outsmarted. Still cursing, he dropped the gun and without prompting, he lifted his hands in the air.

"Get facedown on the ground," Eli instructed. "Hands tucked behind your head—though I'm pretty sure you know how this all works. I'm guessing this isn't your first rodeo."

Eli kicked the guy's weapon away so that he wouldn't be able to reach it, took out a pair of plastic cuffs from his back pocket, and he restrained him while he read him his rights.

"I'm remaining silent," the man snarled.

Eli would do everything possible to change his mind during interrogation. For now, he texted Gunnar to let him know he had the gunman. Something that Gunnar had likely figured out since he had no doubt been watching. Gunnar would send the backup to help haul the man back to the sheriff's office.

Any word from Garcia? Eli added in his text.

Eli didn't have to wait long for a response. His phone vibrated with an incoming call, and he saw Garcia's name on the screen. Maybe this meant Garcia had Remy in custody.

Or not...

When Eli answered the call, he heard Garcia's single word of raw profanity, followed by, "Remy's not here. He got away."

Chapter Thirteen

From the doorway of Kellan's office, Ashlyn just stood back and watched the chaos in the squad room. Gunnar was booking the gunman while Eli was on the phone, barking out orders to the team of Rangers and deputies that he had out looking for Remy.

So far, there'd been so sign of the man.

Since no one had heard the sounds of a vehicle after Remy disappeared into the barn, it meant he'd fled on foot. Ashlyn doubted he'd done that solely because he was so upset over being at Marta's grave. No. Remy had run because there would be charges brought against him.

Maybe murder charges.

After all, someone had murdered the mortician, and right now Remy had the strongest motive for that. With the mortician dead and those files missing, there'd be no proof that Remy had indeed stolen

Marta's body. Well, no proof other than the body itself. But what if it wasn't there?

She immediately shook her head, rethinking that. Remy had been very upset as he stood by that headstone. She'd practically been able to feel his grief, and Ashlyn didn't think he'd be able to fake that.

Ashlyn continued to watch as Gunnar stood with the still-cuffed gunman, and Gunnar motioned for Garcia to follow him. The two deputies led the man not toward lockup but in the direction of the interview room. Maybe that meant the guy was willing to talk. A few minutes later, Gunnar returned with Kellan. Eli quickly ended his call and joined them in Kellan's office.

"The guy's name is Al Waite," Gunnar said. "And you were right about him having a record," he added to Eli. "B&E, assault, drug possession. He's only thirty-one, and he's already spent nearly seven years behind bars."

"Did he say who hired him?" Eli immediately asked.

"No, but you'll be able to press him on that. I put him in interview room one since Dominick and his lawyer are still in the other."

Shortly after she'd arrived back at the sheriff's office, Ashlyn had heard that Kellan was still in interview, but she hadn't known if he was with Oscar or Dominick. She hoped that Dominick would just leave quietly because she wasn't up to another confrontation—with anyone. She just wanted to get all of this resolved so she could get back to the ranch with the baby.

"Waite had a tranquilizer gun on him," Gunnar went on, snagging Ashlyn's attention again.

Eli's head jerked back, and Ashlyn knew the reason for his surprise. Maybe he hadn't gone there to kill Remy after all.

"You think Waite was waiting for Remy to come out of the barn so he could kidnap him?" Ashlyn asked.

"It's looking that way. In addition to the tranquilizer gun, he had some tape and restraints on him."

"But he didn't go closer to the barn when Remy went inside it," Eli said as if thinking out loud. "Unless he didn't see Remy go in."

True. Garcia didn't spot Waite until after he'd told them about Remy leaving the backyard and going to the barn.

"Waite could have been waiting for Remy to come back out, too," Kellan suggested.

That was a possibility as well, but she figured they had all considered something else, and it was Eli who voiced it.

"Remy could have used Waite to distract us so he could get away. And so it would make him look like a potential victim rather than the person who hired Waite."

Both Gunnar and Kellan made sounds of agreement.

"When I moved up behind Waite to take him," Eli went on, "his attention was on the barn. I believe he knew Remy was in there."

And that meant Remy had maybe played them all. Including Waite. The gunman might not have known that the evening would end with his arrest.

"What can you charge Waite with?" she asked.

Gunnar scrubbed his hand over his face. "Parole violation for carrying a weapon. That would send him back to jail to finish out his five-year sentence."

So, not too much time. If Remy had paid him well, that might be enough to set up this ruse. But why?

"If Remy wanted to escape, why didn't he just try to drive off?" she pressed.

"That's what I'll ask Remy when we find him," Eli assured her. He checked his watch. "Let me question Waite, and then I can drive you back to the ranch. Is Cora okay?"

"She's fine. Gloria said she's already tucked in for the night."

Eli nodded. "I'll try to hurry so you can get back to see her."

She wanted to jump at that offer, but more than that, she wanted answers. "Take your time. I want to know who hired him." She looked at Kellan. "I'm guessing Oscar or Dominick didn't make any confessions?"

"Nothing," Kellan answered on a weary sigh. "But then they both know there's only circumstantial evidence against them. Neither of them is running scared like Remy."

Yes, but that didn't mean one of them wasn't guilty.

Eli started out, heading for the interview room, but his phone rang after he'd only made it a few steps. He hesitated for just a couple of seconds when he looked at the screen, and Ashlyn didn't think it was her imagination that he was steeling himself.

"It's the CSIs," Eli relayed to them. He took the call, but this time he didn't put it on speaker.

The moments crawled by, and while she could hear the chatter on the other end of the line, Ashlyn couldn't make out what the caller was saying. Gunnar and Kellan stayed put, too, obviously waiting to hear.

"You're sure?" Eli asked the caller, and he gave a resigned nod before he ended the call. "The Rangers sent in imaging equipment. Ground-penetrating radar." He paused, his gaze locking with Ashlyn's. "There's a body buried beneath the headstone at Remy's place."

A body.

Marta.

Ashlyn hadn't expected the news to hit her as

hard as it did. After all, Remy had told them he'd had her buried there. Still, she'd held on to a thin thread of hope that he'd lied, that Marta was out there somewhere and alive.

"They'll exhume the body," Eli went on, "so that we'll have confirmation."

Yes, that was a legal necessity, but all four of them knew the truth. They hadn't been mistaken about Marta being gunned down in that alley.

"I can take the interview with Waite," Kellan offered.

But Eli shook his head. "You're about to drop on your feet. Get some rest, and I'll have a go at him."

Kellan didn't refuse. "I'll catch a nap in the break room." He looked at Gunnar. "Come and get me if anything breaks."

Gunnar assured him that he would, and Kellan walked out. Eli stayed put, and he caught on to her hand. "Are you okay?"

"I was about to ask you the same thing," she admitted.

He gave a dry smile that didn't make it to his eyes, and he pulled her into his arms. "Having hope can make you end up feeling like you took a punch to the gut, huh?"

Yes, it could.

"I replay that night all the time," he went on, not waiting for her to answer. "I go over all the things I should have done. If I'd just seen how things were going to play out, I could have stopped it. Marta would be alive, and you wouldn't have been shot. In my mind, I undo the mistakes and make it all right."

Ashlyn tightened her grip on him, eased him closer. "I do the same thing. Not just with what went on that night but how I dealt with the aftermath." She looked up at him. "I was wrong to blame you, but you were alive and an easy target."

Eli shrugged, but she knew there was nothing casual or dismissive about it. Her blame had hurt him. Maybe even crushed him. She could see that now, and while it wouldn't go back and undo those scars, she hoped the kiss she brushed on his mouth would help with the healing.

"I'm in love with you, Eli," she said. "I have been for years." Then she winced at his stunned expression. "Yes, I know. The timing sucks." Ashlyn huffed, kissed him again and then eased him back away from her. "Go ahead and talk to Waite. I'll be in the observation room, and when we're done, we can finish this conversation."

Because he didn't budge, she thought he might refuse, but then he cursed, caught on to her hand and headed toward the hall. They were nearly at observation when Dominick and his lawyer came out of the interview room.

Ashlyn groaned before she could stop herself. She was emotionally wrung out, and she was positive that showed on her face. It certainly showed on

Dominick's. Over the past couple of months, she'd seen him angry and combative, but she'd never seen him look exhausted.

"Ashlyn." The weariness was in his voice, too. "My lawyer and I were just going over my statement. I just signed it," he added to Eli.

Eli made a sound that could have meant anything, and he would have moved Ashlyn past them if Dominick hadn't stepped in front of her.

"It's not a good time to annoy me," Eli warned him, and every part of him was dark and dangerous.

Dominick nodded, and if he was bothered by Eli's show of temper, he didn't react. "I only wanted to tell Ashlyn that I was sorry. I can't imagine how stressful the attacks have been for her."

The apology seemed sincere, and she thought that Dominick wanted her to respond with some kind of olive branch of her own. But he didn't wait for that. Motioning for his lawyer to follow him, Dominick walked out.

Just seeing the man leave helped Ashlyn settle some of her nerves. So did the hand that Eli ran down her back. It stilled her. And surprised her. After she'd just dropped the *L*-word bombshell, she'd figured he would try to put some distance between them. At least until after this interview. He didn't. In fact, Eli dropped a quick kiss on her mouth before he left her in observation and went into interview.

"I'm Scott Sanders," the lawyer said, standing. "My client and I want a bail hearing ASAP."

"You and I both know your client won't get bail." Eli sat across from Waite. "He was carrying a gun, which is a violation of his parole. His parole officer has already been contacted."

The lawyer didn't even react to that and instead looked at his phone screen—and frowned.

"I found that gun," Waite insisted. He was a wiry man with beady eyes that darted around as if he expected someone to jump out at him. Maybe he just needed a fix, but Ashlyn couldn't see why anyone would have hired him to go after Remy or anyone else, for that matter.

"You found it," Eli repeated. He couldn't have possibly sounded more skeptical.

"Yeah. In the woods, there," Waite added. Beneath the table, Ashlyn could see his legs fidgeting as much as the rest of him." My car wouldn't start so I started walking, looking for help. That's when I found the gun."

Eli calmly leaned forward, and even though Ashlyn couldn't see his face, she'd bet he was giving Waite a hard glare. "Why didn't you just use your phone to call someone? You had a cell in your pocket."

Waite went stiff, and he looked up at the ceiling as if to find the answer there. Since he obviously didn't, he didn't say anything.

"You had a tranq gun and duct tape on you," Eli went on. "And before you give me some lame excuse to explain those things, I should probably tell you that a deputy sheriff had you under observation from the time you stepped onto the property. He saw enough that you'll be headed back to a cage."

Eli leaned back and waited.

It didn't take long.

"I want a deal," Waite said, and he shook off the grip that his lawyer put on his arm.

Eli didn't jump on that, either. He just took his time. "What kind of deal?"

"I tell you what I know, and I don't go back to jail. I can't go back there, man. You gotta give me a break."

"I don't have to give you anything," Eli assured him. "But if you tell me what you know, I'll consider it. I'll even put in a good word for you with the DA."

She hadn't thought it possible, but Waite's fidgeting got even worse. "Okay," Waite said after giving that some thought. He shook off his lawyer again. "Someone paid me to go out there. I don't know who," Waite quickly added.

"And what exactly were you supposed to do?" Eli pressed.

"Just grab the guy and drop him off at that old abandoned gas station up the road. I wasn't supposed to hurt him or nothing. It wasn't even like a serious crime or anything."

"You were supposed to kidnap a man, tranq him, tie him up and put duct tape on his mouth. Sounds plenty serious to me." Eli sat back again and waited. "I'll bet it sounds even worse to the man you were supposed to kidnap."

Waite's eyes darted around. "Well, I didn't do it, and I'd changed my mind before you even got there and arrested me. I wasn't going through with it."

"Right," Eli grumbled. "Who's the *someone* who hired you to do this? Give me a name, and I'll push to get you a deal."

"No," the lawyer blurted out. "Don't tell him anything…not until he puts it in writing. You can't trust him. He'll lie to get the information he wants."

"I'll put you back in a cage to get the information I want," Eli calmly answered. "But I just offered you a deal, and I meant it. Give me a name, and if it pans out, you won't be charged with a parole violation."

Waite kept his gaze nailed to Eli's, and when he opened his mouth, Ashlyn automatically moved closer to the glass. Her heart was pounding now. Her breath, held. Maybe they would finally know the truth.

However, before Waite could say anything, the lawyer's phone dinged with a text message. Since she could clearly see Sanders, she thought maybe there was relief, as if this was something he'd been waiting for.

Yes, definitely relief.

Ashlyn saw even more of it when he silently read whatever was on his phone screen. Sanders showed the text to Waite, his eyes darting across the message, and he swallowed hard. Every drop of color seemed to drain from his face.

"No deal," Waite said. His voice was suddenly as shaky as he was. "I'm not saying another word to you."

Chapter Fourteen

Eli had already used every curse word he knew. Multiple times. And he would have used them all over again if he'd thought it would help. It wouldn't. No matter how hard he'd pressed Waite, the man had just clammed up.

Or rather he'd been threatened if he continued to speak.

Eli knew that in his gut.

Waite had been ready to spill. Eli was absolutely certain of that. But the confession had been nixed because of whatever was in the text that Waite's lawyer had shown him. Now, even after all that cursing and the phone calls, Eli still didn't have proof of who'd sent that text.

Eli reined in any urges to belt out more profanity, and he stopped pacing when Ashlyn came into the kitchen. The moment they'd gotten back to Jack's house, she'd gone into the bedroom to check on Cora, and judging from her expression and the fact that it was a short check, everything seemed to be okay there. He figured her raised eyebrow was for him and not anything going on with the baby. Ashlyn wanted an update on the case, especially since the danger was breathing down their necks.

"Nothing," he volunteered, keeping his voice at a whisper since Gunnar was already asleep on the sofa. "It was a no-go on getting the lawyer to reveal any info about that text."

Of course, Eli hadn't expected anything different. After all, the lawyer could claim it was client-attorney privilege, but it still riled him to the core. Waite and the lawyer were on the same payroll, and Eli wanted the murdering SOB who was paying them behind bars.

"What about the tails you had on Oscar and Dominick?" Ashlyn asked. "Did they see anything?"

"Oh, yeah." And that was the second source of Eli's extreme frustration. "According to the deputy on Oscar, she saw him use his phone right about the time of the text which means he could have been the one to tell Waite to shut up. Of course, Oscar isn't willing to just hand over his phone, so I'm having to work on a court order to get that, too."

He'd get the court order, but if Oscar was truly behind this, then he'd likely used a burner, something that couldn't be traced. Something that Oscar would have already ditched.

"What about Dominick?" Ashlyn walked closer, and she slid her hands into the back pockets of her jeans. "Did he come up with the receipts for the renovations?"

"More or less. There are receipts, all right, for the nursery redo, but we'll have to check and make sure they're legit. I still think that's way too much cash for a single room."

Proving that, though, wouldn't be easy, and like the text, it could be impossible to get to the truth. Someone like Dominick could have easily paid a contractor to falsify receipts.

Since Eli didn't want to dump that bad news on Ashlyn, he changed the subject. "Is Cora okay?"

She nodded. "Whoever brought in the crib put it in the spare room where Gloria's asleep."

"Good. It's best if Cora's not alone in the bedroom."

The moment Eli said the words, he wanted to wince. On the surface, it was an innocent thing to say, but Ashlyn and he weren't anywhere near the "surface." There was the blasted attraction. And more. It was what she'd said to him earlier.

I'm in love with you, Eli.

That was definitely deep stuff, and Eli knew he couldn't continue to step around it. However, before he even had the chance to bring it up, his phone buzzed to indicate he had a call. He scowled when he saw the name on the screen and immediately showed it to Ashlyn.

Remy.

Since Eli definitely wanted to talk to him, he motioned for Ashlyn to follow him to the bedroom he'd been using. That way, the conversation wouldn't wake up Gloria, the baby or Gunnar. Eli shut the door and put the call on speaker.

"Hold on a second, Remy," Eli told the man, and he texted dispatch so they could try to trace the call. "Where are you?" Eli demanded once he'd done that.

Remy didn't jump to answer, though. It took him several long moments. "I'm in hiding. Someone wants to kill me. That's why I sneaked out of the barn and went on the run."

Eli huffed. "You're sure you didn't run because you're guilty of the attacks?"

"No." Remy didn't hesitate that time. "I didn't have anything to do with them, I swear."

"Don't hold your breath waiting for me to believe you about that. You stole Marta's body, then hid it, and you're on the run from the law. That's three strikes in my book, and it doesn't add up to someone I intend to trust. Now, where the hell are you?"

"I don't want to tell you because I don't trust you, either. You haven't done your job and fixed this. Someone was following me, and after everything that's happened, that person might want me dead, too. Who's doing this, Eli? Who wants to murder us?"

Eli wasn't buying into Remy's denial, but the man certainly sounded afraid. Of course, fear could be faked, and Remy had a strong motive for wanting to kill him. Maybe Remy had stretched that motive to include Ashlyn as well, but if so, Remy was also coming after the baby, since she was in the middle of this mess.

"You need to arrest whoever's trying to kill us. Until you do that, I'm protecting myself, and it starts by not telling you where I am. Find him, Eli, or I will," Remy warned him, and he ended the call.

Eli groaned, and even though he knew Remy hadn't been on the line long enough, he called dispatch anyway. "Nothing," Eli had to relay to Ashlyn once he had his answer. "They weren't able to trace it."

Frustrated, he put his phone back in his pocket and mentally replayed everything Remy had just told him. Which wasn't much. However, if Remy did indeed try to play cop and find their attacker, then he could put himself right in the path of a killer. If Remy wasn't the killer, that is. If he was, then his call had merely been an attempt to make himself look innocent.

It hadn't worked.

He intended to keep the man on his suspect list. Eli looked up when he felt Ashlyn touch his arm, and he immediately saw the fresh concern in her eyes. He knew that she just wanted this to be over. So did he. But Remy was right about one thing. Eli did need to arrest the snake who kept putting them in danger. So far, they'd gotten lucky by getting away from the gunfire, but their luck might not hold out much longer.

Ashlyn kept her gaze on him, and after a few seconds, Eli didn't think her expression was only one of concern. Well, it wasn't solely about the attacks anyway. That worry was there all right, but there was also something else.

That *I'm in love with you.*

"I know what you're going to say," Ashlyn blurted out before Eli could broach that subject. "You don't want me to be in love with you, and I get that. Believe me, I get it," she added in a frustrated mumble. "If I could change how I feel about you, I would."

Okay, that spelled it out for him. She wasn't any happier about this than he was. But then she shook her head. "That's not exactly true," she amended. "I probably wouldn't change things in the feelings department."

"You should," he insisted right off. "I'm bad news, Ashlyn. I can't make the past go away."

Her gaze came back to him, and she gave him a blank stare. "There were some good things in that past. And yes, I know it's hard to see the good what with all the bad. I hung on to that bad for a very long time, blaming you for something that wasn't your fault." She stepped closer, laying her palm on his chest. "It wasn't your fault."

He wanted to believe that. Better yet, Eli wanted her to believe it, but the hurt would always be there.

And apparently so would the attraction.

Certain parts of his body took her touch as some sort of signal that more should happen to tap into that attraction. Eli was almost certain he could have resisted, almost, if Ashlyn hadn't come up on her toes and put her mouth close to his. She didn't actually kiss him.

So Eli kissed her.

Even though he knew there was a high chance of regretting this, Eli dragged her to him and finished what Ashlyn had started. And there it was. That kick of heat so strong that he wondered how the heck he'd ever resisted her in the first place.

Ashlyn melted right into the kiss. She melted right against him, too. With her hand trapped between them, she pressed her body to his, a reminder of just how well they fit together.

Eli deepened the kiss, letting it fan the fire even more until the kiss and the body contact weren't enough. He needed more, and judging from the way Ashlyn was struggling to touch more of him, she felt the same way.

Her free hand slid down his back, urging him

closer and closer, and the sound that she made in her throat was one of pure desire. Eli hadn't needed anything else to rev him up, but that did it.

He shoved up her top, lowered his head and kissed the tops of her breasts. All in all, that was a good way to take things to next level, but soon it wasn't enough, either, and Eli found himself backing Ashlyn across the room. First, he locked the door, and then he led her in the direction of the bed—while he kissed her again.

They fell back, sinking into the feather mattress while the sides of it swelled around them. Everything around them was soft. Except for Eli. And he could feel his body going steely hard.

Ashlyn went after his neck, kissing him there, while she fought with his shirt to get the buttons undone. It wasn't easy since Eli was waging his own battle against her clothes. He finally managed to peel off her top, then he pushed down her bra so he could kiss her breasts.

She stopped with his buttons, arched her back to move her breasts even closer to his mouth, and she made another of those sounds of pleasure. Since it was something she obviously liked, Eli lingered there a few more seconds until the urgency kicked in again, and Ashlyn went after his zipper. As soon as she got it down, she slid her hand down into his boxers.

He could have sworn his eyes crossed. It certainly robbed him of what little breath he had. Eli ground his teeth and let her touch spear the pleasure through him.

Man, he wanted Ashlyn, and he wanted her now.

Eli had to push her hand away so he could get his jeans unzipped. Ashlyn finally gave up her touching quest and helped him with that. Together, they shimmied off her jeans. Her panties, too.

"Now," she insisted.

He definitely wanted to give her "now," but Eli kissed her again and skimmed his hand from her breasts down to the inside of her thighs. That was pleasure for both of them, because Ashlyn ground herself against him, seeking the cure for the pressure cooker of heat that they'd built together.

She repeated her "now" while she groped the waist of his jeans to get them down. As much as Eli was enjoying the kissing, he knew it was time to cut the foreplay and finish this. He got off his boots and jeans and remembered to take the condom from his wallet before he tossed his clothes and boxers onto the floor.

He kept it gentle as he slipped inside her and even stilled to give Ashlyn a moment to adjust to the pressure of him filling her. But Eli quickly learned that it wasn't gentleness she wanted. Ashlyn hooked her leg around his lower back and gave him a push while she lifted her hips to meet his thrust.

Eli took things from there. It was obvious she

didn't want him to treat her like someone fragile or broken, so he didn't hold back. He gave her, and himself, exactly what they needed. The movement came harder. Faster. And with each plunge inside her, it took them closer and closer to the edge.

Ashlyn went over first, the climax rippling through her and gripping on to him like a fist. After that, Eli couldn't have hung on even if he'd wanted to. His body needed release.

And *he* needed Ashlyn.

Those ripples of her body coaxed and pushed him until Eli buried his face against her neck and let himself go.

ASHLYN HADN'T REMEMBERED to keep her scars hidden away. That was a first for her, but then sex with Eli apparently could rid her of any self-consciousness, including what she had about those scars from her gunshot wounds.

Of course, he'd already seen them because she'd shown them to him. However, that'd been a quick glimpse, and it would likely be a whole lot more than that now what with her naked.

The moment that Eli moved off her and dropped on his back next to her on the bed, Ashlyn reached for the cover to drape it over her body. Eli stopped her, though, by catching on to her hand. First, he frowned, and then he kissed her.

Before he looked at those scars.

His frown deepened for a moment before he leaned down, kissed them, too, and he got up, gathering up his jeans and boxers before he headed into the adjoining bathroom. Only then did Ashlyn release the breath she'd been holding.

Thank goodness, the scars hadn't brought back the memories of that awful night, and there'd been enough heat left in his eyes to tell her that they hadn't been a turnoff, either. What could be a turnoff, though, was when he had time to think about this, because he would almost certainly see it as a mistake.

And maybe the timing exactly was.

After all, they had plenty they should be doing to get to the bottom of who was trying to kill them. But it was hard for Ashlyn to regret her finally making love to Eli. In fact, she doubted anything would make her regret that. Including a broken heart.

Eli wasn't in love with her. Ashlyn was pretty sure if he had been that he would have said something about it by now, and it was probably bothering him that he didn't feel the same way about her that she did him. That would cause him plenty of regrets, too, but she doubted he'd be able to deal with his feelings or anything else personal until the danger was over.

Remembering that danger, Ashlyn got up so she could get dressed and check on the baby. She hadn't heard any sounds coming from across the hall, and if Cora had indeed woken up, Gloria would have certainly let her know. Still, she wanted to see her daughter, and maybe that would help settle the nerves that were starting to jangle inside her.

And speaking of jangled nerves, Ashlyn got more of them when Eli came out of the bathroom. He'd put on his jeans, but since he was shirtless, she got a nice view of his toned and perfect chest. Too bad she hadn't taken the time to savor that, but then making love with him had seemed too urgent for foreplay.

He stopped in the doorway of the bathroom and combed his gaze over her. It wasn't exactly regret that she saw on his face, but there was some concern.

"Please don't tell me you're sorry this happened," Ashlyn told him before he could say anything.

His eyes stayed on her. "Well, I am sorry you're dressed." And he flashed her a smile that warmed her all over again. If a mere smile could do that, she figured another kiss would land them back in bed. However, there wasn't time for that, because Eli's phone buzzed.

"Kellan," he relayed to her after he glanced at the screen. Eli put the call on speaker and laid his phone on the bed so he could get dressed.

"Everything okay there?" Kellan said the moment he was on the line.

"So far. Please tell me you've got good news."

"Some. The CSIs found Waite's prints in Hamby's car. That's enough for me to threaten him with accessory to attempted murder. His lawyer will come back in first thing in the morning so I'll have a chat with Waite then."

Good. And attempted murder just might be enough to get the man talking. If so, that could lead to Waite giving them the name of the person who'd hired him.

"I want to be there when you question Waite," Eli insisted.

Kellan didn't argue with that. "I'll let you know where it's all set up, but considering the other attacks, I think you should leave Ashlyn there. I can send out a pair of the reserve deputies to stay with her."

Ashlyn didn't like the idea of Eli going out there and opening himself up to another attack. Nor did she especially care for being with the reserve deputies. Still, she doubted Eli would agree to letting her go back to the sheriff's office with him.

Eli had just finished putting on his shirt when his phone dinged with an incoming call. "Gotta go," he told Kellan. "One of the hands is trying to ring in."

Hearing that automatically kicked up Ashlyn's pulse, but she reminded herself that this could be just an update since the hands were keeping watch of the grounds.

"Eli, this is Jeremy," the hand said after Eli had answered.

Jeremy Cranston, one of the top hands. Ashlyn knew him, and the last time she'd seen him, he'd been in the front pasture.

"There's a car that's stopped just up from the ranch road," Jeremy went on. "The headlights are on high so I can't see through the glare to get a glimpse of who's inside."

"Can you read the license plate?" Eli asked.

"Sure." And Jeremy rattled that off to Eli.

"Thanks," Eli told him. "Hold on just a minute while I have dispatch run the plates—"

"The car's moving," Jeremy blurted out, his voice louder now and edged with even more alarm. "Fast…hell! Eli, the car just broke through the fence and is headed right for us."

Chapter Fifteen

Eli knew in his gut that this wasn't just some driver who'd gotten turned around. No. This was probably the start of another attack. A stupid one. Because in addition to Gunnar and him, all the hands were armed and ready for something like this.

"Make sure the baby is okay," Eli told Ashlyn, though he knew that Cora was fine. Still, he wanted Ashlyn to stay put. Best to not have her anywhere near the front of the house until he made sure that she wasn't in danger. "If you hear anything, go in the room with Cora and Gloria and make sure all of you stay down."

She gave a shaky nod and didn't question him as to what he meant about hearing "anything." Ashlyn knew they'd all be listening for the sound of gunshots.

Because he thought they could both use it, Eli brushed a quick kiss on Ashlyn's mouth and headed for the front door. "Wake up," he told Gunnar as he hurried past him.

The deputy did, and he automatically drew his gun. "What's wrong?"

Eli looked out the small window on the side of the door, and he cursed. There was indeed a car coming across the pasture. A dark sedan. It tore through the section of wood fence and came right toward the house.

"Want me to try to shoot the driver?" Gunnar asked.

Eli considered it. Heck, he wanted to do it himself. But he didn't know what they were up against.

"Hold off just a second," Eli told him, and he took aim. Gunnar did the same at the other side window.

The car jolted to a stop about ten yards from the house, but Eli didn't have any better luck than Jeremy had at seeing inside the vehicle. The high beams were cutting through the darkness, though, and it meant if someone got out, Eli and Gunnar would have no trouble spotting them. However, someone could possibly sneak out of the trunk, so Eli took out his phone to warn Jeremy about that, but before he could do that his phone buzzed again with a call.

Remy.

Eli wanted to let it go to voice mail because he didn't want the distraction of another round of conversation with the man. But something in his gut told him to answer. The moment he did and put the call on speaker, he heard Remy's frantic voice pour through the room.

"Don't shoot me," Remy said. "I have a hostage."

Eli hadn't thought his muscles could go any tighter, but he'd been wrong. "What hostage?" Eli demanded.

There were some muffled sounds. Maybe a struggle going on. "I'll kill you if you move again," Remy growled, and Eli was pretty sure the man wasn't talking to him.

"Who's your hostage?" Eli ordered Remy, and he tried not to think the worst. That maybe Remy had taken one of the hands or an innocent bystander.

"I've got Dominick," Remy spat out. "And if he keeps trying to get his hands untied or kick me again, he'll die."

"Dominick?" Eli heard Ashlyn repeat. He glanced over his shoulder to make sure she had stayed put. She had. Ashlyn was in the hall just outside the door where Cora was sleeping. She looked shaky but confused, too. Eli was on the same page with her. What the hell was going on here?

"Why do you have Dominick?" Eli pressed, and that was just the first of many questions he had for Remy.

Eli turned his attention back to Remy's vehicle. Or rather to the vehicle that had crashed through the fence. The odds were that Remy was indeed inside. Maybe Dominick, too. But Eli also knew this could be a trap and that Remy's call could be just a distraction.

There could be gunmen inside that car, and they

could be waiting to come out shooting. The fact that they'd gotten this close to the house riled Eli all the way to his bones. This wasn't like the other attack on the road. It was worse. Because this time Cora could be caught in the crosshairs of a killer.

"Text Jeremy and tell him to keep an eye on the trunk," Eli mouthed to Gunnar, and the deputy immediately took out his phone to do that. "And then let Kellan know what happened."

"You're gonna listen to me," Remy carried on, "or Dominick will die. So help me, I'll put a bullet in him."

Remy certainly sounded desperate enough to do something that stupid, but it still didn't make sense to Eli. "I'm listening," Eli assured him. "Now, tell me what you want and why you have Dominick."

"I don't want Marta's body moved," Remy insisted. "I don't want anyone touching her."

Eli listened for any hint that the demand didn't ring true, but it did. Well, it did if Remy had gone off the deep end. Since the man had been acting more erratic than usual, that was possible.

"You need to stop this idiot!" Dominick shouted, and the sound of his voice didn't just come over the phone line. Eli heard it from within the car. Of course, it could be some kind of recording, something meant to be a decoy or distraction, but Eli was starting to believe this was what it appeared to be. Remy losing all control and taking a hostage.

Except there was a problem with that.

"How the hell did you manage to take Dominick?" Eli asked Remy. "Better yet, *why* did you take him?"

"I needed leverage," Remy answered almost immediately. "I knew you'd listen to me if I had a hostage, so when I saw Dominick coming out of the sheriff's office, I followed him."

"The idiot used a stun gun on me," Dominick snarled. The man's anger certainly seemed genuine. "He tied my hands when he got me in the car and then drove around crying," Dominick added with some disgust.

"I can't lose Marta," Remy snarled back, but then it sounded as if a hoarse sob tore from his mouth. "I lost her once, and that can't happen again."

Eli doubted the best response to that would be to remind Remy that Marta was already dead. Obviously, the man was well past the point of reasoning.

"Whose car do you have?" Eli pressed. "Because the one in the yard isn't yours." And he needed to make sure it wasn't some kind of decoy.

"It belongs to a friend. I had him come and get me after I ran from the barn."

"Is that friend in the car with you now?" Eli added.

"No, it's just Dominick and me. Now, here's what you're going to do," Remy went on without waiting for Eli to respond. "You're gonna call Marta's dad and get it *in writing* that he won't try to move her. I've been trying to reason with him, but he blocked my calls."

Eli didn't blame Gus for doing that. After all, Remy had stolen Gus's daughter's body.

"When you get Gus on the line, I want to talk to him," Remy went on. "I want to hear him say that he agrees to it, that he'll let her stay near me. Then he can put it in writing. I want that done right now."

As demands went, it wasn't an especially hard one. Or rather it wouldn't be if he could get in touch with Gus right away. Still, even if Remy got that guarantee, he had a hostage. And he'd committed a serious crime. Eli was going to have to defuse the situation and arrest the man.

"Okay," Eli said. "We'll try to call Gus right now." Since Eli didn't want to take his focus off the car, he motioned for Gunnar to do that.

Even though Eli's pulse was drumming in his ears, he could still hear the ringing sound when Gunnar tried the call. Eli dragged in his breath, waiting, but Gus didn't answer.

Hell.

This just got a whole lot harder.

"Gus didn't pick up," Eli relayed to Remy, "but I know he'll agree to this. He wouldn't want to see a man hurt."

"It has to be in writing!" Remy yelled. "That's the only way I let Dominick go. Try to call Gus again, and keep calling until you speak to him."

Eli nodded for Gunnar to keep trying. The deputy would, but while they waited, Eli was going to have to do something to defuse this. Thankfully, he had some backup. In the distance he could see a vehicle approaching on the ranch road. Kellan. At least he hoped it was. But if not, maybe this vehicle wouldn't break through the fence, too.

"You don't need Dominick as a hostage," Eli told Remy. "You've got a gun, and I can't risk you firing shots this close to the house. That's enough to keep you safe so you can let Dominick go."

"He's staying put," Remy snapped. "I don't trust you."

The feeling was mutual. Of course, Eli wasn't certain he could trust Dominick, either, but that was something he'd have to work out later.

Gunnar tried Gus's number again, and Eli finally released the breath he'd been holding when he heard the man answer.

"Tell him what's going on," Eli instructed Gunnar, and he turned back to Remy to let him know they'd reached Marta's father.

Before Eli could do that, though, he heard something he definitely didn't want to hear.

A gunshot.

ASHLYN HAD NO trouble realizing someone had just fired a gun, and it sent a jolt of fear and terror through her. After the attacks, she'd become too familiar with that horrible sound. And she knew what it meant.

They were in danger again.

Turning to go to Cora, she was about to shout for Eli to get down. He was right at the little window by the door, and a bullet could easily go through the glass and kill him. But Eli mumbled something to Gunnar, something she didn't catch, and the deputy turned and ran toward her. Gunnar shoved his phone into his jeans pocket, took her by the arm and moved her into the open doorway of the bedroom that Eli had been using.

"Go into the bathroom," Gunnar told her.

She frantically shook her head. "I need to make sure Cora's okay," Ashlyn insisted, fighting to get out of his grip.

"I'll do that. You go into the bathroom."

Ashlyn didn't do as he'd ordered. She stood there, watching, and she had to fight against all her maternal instincts to go with the deputy. She was the one who should be checking on her child. She should be there to protect Cora if she needed it. However, Ashlyn could see into the room when Gunnar eased open the door. Gloria was already out of bed, and she had a sleeping Cora clutched to her.

"Go in there," Gunnar instructed, tipping his head to the attached bath. "Lock the door behind you. Then, get in the tub with her and stay down until I tell you it's okay to come out."

It was a small claw-foot tub, only large enough for one person, but Ashlyn thought it was deep enough that it would protect Cora and Gloria if someone fired another bullet.

She prayed it was enough.

Gloria hurried into the bathroom and disappeared out of sight. Ashlyn's fear spiked even higher, and the jolt of adrenaline she got made it nearly impossible to stay put. She wanted to take her baby and run to safety, but she had to remind herself that right now staying put could be the right thing to do.

Ashlyn glanced back at the bathroom that Eli had used earlier. It was just as small as the other one, and instead of a tub, it had a shower. She hadn't gone inside it, but she was certain it wouldn't have the space for Gloria, Cora and her.

"Remy?" Eli shouted, and she realized he was talking into his phone. "Are you there?" If Remy answered, she couldn't hear what the man said.

"What's happening?" Ashlyn asked Gunnar when he came back to her. "Did Remy fire that shot?"

"We're not sure yet. It looks as if Remy's taken Dominick hostage, and it sounded as if some kind of struggle was going on in the car."

Oh, mercy. Dominick a hostage? One that Remy had brought here to the ranch. That was more than enough for her to process, but Ashlyn hadn't missed Gunnar's "looks as if Remy's taken Dominick hostage."

"You think Remy could be lying?" she asked.

Gunnar lifted his shoulder. "Remy's definitely not thinking straight, and he said he wants to use Dominick to get Gus to agree not to move Marta." Gunnar didn't look at her though when he spoke. He kept his attention nailed to Eli.

So if Remy had told them the truth, this was about Marta and maybe didn't have anything to do with the other attacks. That didn't mean, though, that one of them couldn't be hurt.

"I need a gun," Ashlyn told him. "Just in case Remy or someone else gets inside the house." Because she had a really bad feeling about this.

She could see the debate going on in Gunnar's eyes over her request, but he finally reached down, took out a small weapon from his boot holster, and he handed it to her.

"Giving you this doesn't mean I want you out in the open. If you don't stay down, you'll have to answer to Eli. So will I," he added under his ragged breath.

Ashlyn knew that was true, but if they did have to answer to Eli, that would mean this had all been a false alarm. That the only danger was to Dominick and not any of them.

When Ashlyn started across the hall toward Gloria and Cora, he stopped her again. "Eli wants you to hunker down in the shower," Gunnar reminded her.

"And I need to prevent anyone from getting to Cora," she snapped.

Ashlyn made sure her tone and expression let him know that she wasn't going to budge on this. She moved into the doorway of Cora's and Gloria's room. That way, she could easily hear them in the bathroom, and she could keep an eye on the window opposite the bed.

Eli had told her that all the doors and windows were wired into the security system, but she wanted to be there if someone tried to break in. If that did indeed happen, Ashlyn consoled herself with the reminder that Gloria had locked the bathroom. That meant an intruder would not only have to get past her but also break down the door.

Gunnar huffed, cursed and then glanced back at Eli, who was still by the front door. Eli hadn't moved, and there hadn't been any other shots, but he was clearly still standing guard.

"Remy?" Eli shouted again. Like before, he got no response that Ashlyn could hear.

"Maybe Remy shot Dominick," Ashlyn said.

"Maybe," Gunnar agreed. "Or else Dominick got the gun from Remy and turned it on him."

That was possible, but if so, then why hadn't Dominick just come out of the vehicle? She was certain he hadn't, or Eli would have already told Gunnar.

"I'll see what I can find out," Gunnar told her, and he gave her a warning glance to stay put before he hurried back to the front door next to Eli.

Ashlyn wanted to hear their conversation, but she didn't want to move any farther away from Cora and the bedroom window. So she stood there, the gun gripped in her hand, and she waited. She could tell from Gunnar's expression that he didn't have good news when he came back to her.

"Neither Dominick nor Remy is responding," he said. "Either Remy turned off his phone or it's not working."

Ashlyn had no idea which of those could be true, but it was possible the shot she'd heard had damaged the phone. "What happens now?" she asked.

"Kellan's here in the cruiser, and he's about to drive closer so he can try to see in Remy's car. If Remy killed Dominick, accidentally or otherwise, he might be too scared to come out."

True. Or Remy could be lying in wait to gun down Kellan or anyone else who approached him. If the man truly wasn't thinking straight, then there was no telling what he would do.

"Is there any way of knowing where the shot went?" she pressed. Ashlyn hadn't heard it hit the house, but there were plenty of ranch hands patrolling the grounds. She hoped it hadn't hit one of them.

Gunnar shook his head. "The windshield on the car is intact, but it's possible the shot went out the back. Kellan's not going to let this drag on," he added. "He's already called for more cruisers, and when they get here, they can box Remy in."

Since the cruisers were bullet-resistant, that would hopefully mean Remy wouldn't be able to fire a shot into the house. Also, if he lowered his window to try to do that, Kellan or one of the hands would almost certainly take him out.

Ashlyn hated the thought of someone being killed, especially just yards away from her baby, but Remy might not give them a choice. If he'd truly lost his mind, then there might not be any turning back from this for him.

Gunnar went back to the front, taking up position on the other side of the door from Eli. Ashlyn kept her attention on them, and that's why she didn't miss when Eli glanced back at her. Their eyes connected, and she could almost feel his worry and regret. He would blame himself for not being able to stop this, blame himself for not realizing just how close to the edge that Remy had been.

Eli's gaze slashed back to the window when there was another sound. Not a gunshot, thank goodness. This was a screech of tires, and for a moment she thought it was Kellan moving in with one of the cruisers.

But no.

Ashlyn's heart jumped to her throat as she saw Eli's and Gunnar's reactions. The two bolted away from the door, both of them running in her direction.

And the car crashed through the front of the house.

ELI WAS CURSING and praying at the same time. There'd been only seconds to react. Seconds between the time Remy had gunned the engine and used his car as a battering ram to tear into the house.

The front of the car did plenty of damage, breaking down the front door and shattering windows. And setting off the security alarm, which immediately started to blare. If the crash hadn't woken up the baby, that would certainly do it, and despite everything else going on, Eli added a prayer that the little girl wouldn't be scared.

Ashlyn and Gunnar took aim at the car, and while Eli appreciated their quick backup, he wanted Ashlyn away from this. Well, as far away as she could get, which would mean going in with Cora and Gloria. For now, though, Eli used his phone to turn off the security alarms so he could hear.

He heard all right. The sounds of the car engine crackling from the impact. Wood and glass falling. But beneath all of that, he also heard the moans. Someone was hurt. Hopefully, Remy. Eli didn't have any sympathy whatsoever for the man since he'd endangered not only his hostage but everyone in the house.

The moaning picked up a notch, and then the front passenger's door of the car creaked open. Dominick stuck out his head, and since the lights were still on in what was left of the house, Eli had no trouble seeing the blood on the man's head. It looked as if he'd hit it during the collisions.

"Remy set a fire inside the car," Dominick said, and his voice was a mix of pain, fear and anger.

Eli had already noticed the smoke, but he'd thought that had come from the crash. Apparently, though, Remy was determined to do even more damage than he already had.

"Let Kellan know about the fire," Eli told Gunnar. Kellan would almost certainly be approaching the vehicle, and he'd need to be aware what he was up against.

"Is Remy alive?" Eli asked Dominick. He didn't go to the man to help him out of the car and wouldn't until he was positive that Dominick hadn't had some part in this.

Dominick opened his mouth to answer, and then he cursed and groaned. A moment later, Eli saw why Dominick had had that reaction. He got out of the car, and Remy was right behind him.

Remy had a gun pointed at Dominick's head.

Hell. They still had a hostage situation on their hands, and the smoke from the car was getting worse, which meant if there was indeed a fire, it could soon spread into the house. Worse, Kellan wouldn't be able to do anything about that fire as long as Remy had Dominick. Of course, his brother might be able to get a clean shot to take out Remy, and if so, that would put an end to this.

Remy staggered out of the car, and Eli could see that he, too, had a head injury. There was a line of blood snaking down his temple all the way to his jaw, but Remy didn't even seem to notice it. His face was tight with rage and determination. Not a good mix when it came to an out-of-control armed man who seemed hell-bent on doing as much damage as possible.

"Get in the room with Cora," Eli told Ashlyn. Thankfully, she did move but only into the doorway of the bedroom. He would have preferred her to be in the bathroom, but at least she wasn't in the direct line of fire.

Gunnar and Eli took cover, too, both of them scrambling behind the sofa. It wouldn't give them much protection if Remy started shooting, but Eli hadn't given up on reasoning with the man. Maybe that wasn't even possible, but he had to try especially since Kellan was going to be tied up trying to deal with the car.

Behind him, he could hear Cora crying. Could also hear Gloria trying to soothe her.

"Remy, you need to put down your gun," Eli warned him. "We have a baby here, and you could hurt her."

"That baby is my granddaughter," Dominick spat out. He angled his narrowed eyes back at Remy, who now had him in a choke hold. "So help me, if you put one scratch on her, I will kill you."

Remy didn't have a reaction to that, either. He seemed to be in shock as he forced Dominick through the debris from the crash and into the living room. However, Eli rethought that "shock" diagnosis when Remy positioned himself so that his own back was to the wall. It would make it much harder for Kellan to get off that shot. Ditto for Gunnar and Eli. Right now, neither of them could fire because they would almost certainly hit Dominick.

"You need to stop this, Sergeant Slater," Dominick spat out, saying "Sergeant Slater" as if it were the profanity he added after his demand. "You need to kill this lunatic before he does any more damage."

"And you need to stay quiet," Eli told him. It definitely wouldn't help if Dominick agitated Remy even more than he already was.

Dominick glared at Eli and gave him a look that could have frozen hell. Apparently, the man wasn't going to make this easy, so Eli needed to try to defuse this as fast as he could.

Through the gaping hole in the front of the house, Eli saw Kellan and one of the hands inching toward the car. Since the smoke was still spewing from it, maybe they'd be able to deal with that. If Remy let them, that is. If Remy saw them, he might try to shoot them. And that's why Eli had to keep Remy occupied.

"Before you crashed your car into the house, I had Gus on the phone," Eli told him. Not a lie but what he would say next would be. "He agreed not to move Marta's body, and yes, he'll put that in writing."

Gus would probably agree to it only to appease Remy enough to have him put an end to this, but Eli was betting there was no way Gus was going to let Marta's body stay where it was.

Remy didn't say anything, but his gaze continued to fire around the room and toward the car. His eyes were wild, and his hand was shaking. Clearly, he wasn't in control, which made this situation even more dangerous.

Kellan leaned into the smoking car, and using his hat, he batted at the flames. Eli couldn't tell if he'd managed to put out the fire because there was still plenty of smoke. Smoke that was seeping into the house.

"I need a car or truck so I can get out of here," Remy finally said.

Eli huffed. Well, at least it was a demand he could work with. A demand that didn't make sense, though. "Why'd you crash your own car if that's what you wanted?"

Remy shook his head, and yeah, he was dazed. "I didn't intend on doing that. It just happened."

"I was trying to get away from him," Dominick volunteered, "and the idiot jammed his foot on the accelerator."

So that hadn't been part of the plan. Of course, neither had Remy holding Dominick at gunpoint in the living room.

"Obviously, we're not dealing with a bright bulb here," Dominick added in an enraged grumble.

Remy might have been dazed, but he didn't care much for Dominick's insult, and he ground the gun even harder against Dominick's head. "I want a car or truck," Remy repeated, and his words were suddenly as fierce as his expression. "Get it now. I know Kellan's out there, and I can use his cruiser."

Eli nodded. "That can be arranged. I'll have Kellan bring in the keys."

"No," Remy snapped. He glanced out at his car again, and even though Kellan and the hands were no longer in sight, Eli knew they were nearby and waiting to respond.

Dominick huffed. "Like I said, he's not very bright. You'll need the keys, moron," he added, tossing Remy another look from over his shoulder.

Eli wished the man would just shut up, because that put a new layer of rage on Remy's face. "Tell Kellan to leave the keys in the ignition of the cruiser," Remy ordered. "I want the engine running and ready to go. And I want her."

Remy looked past the sofa, past Eli, his attention going into the hall. And Eli's stomach went to his knees, because he knew that Remy was talking about Ashlyn.

"I'll take her instead of Dominick," Remy went on. "She's not as likely to put up a fight, and I'm betting Kellan or you won't fire any shots at me if I've got Ashlyn with me."

"You're not taking Ashlyn," Eli snapped, though he wasn't sure how he managed to speak with everything churning even harder inside him.

Remy's gaze slashed straight to Eli's. "Then I start shooting. You don't want that to happen because like you said, the kid could get hurt. I'm betting Ashlyn will come with me to stop that from happening."

"I will," Ashlyn said.

Eli didn't look back at her. He didn't want to take his attention off Remy, but he wanted to give her a back-off warning. No way was Eli going to let her leave with Remy. In the man's state of mind, he could kill her.

"Take me hostage," Eli insisted. "Kellan and Gunnar won't fire if I'm with you."

Eli could see Remy considering that. And he also saw him dismiss it. "I want Ashlyn. She's likely to give me less trouble than you would."

Yes, she was less likely because she wouldn't be able to defend herself against Remy, who was much larger than she was. Which was another reason why she wasn't leaving with him.

"I won't be armed," Eli said, trying again to reason with Remy. "I'd leave my gun here."

Again, Remy considered that, and this time there wasn't an immediate dismissal. Not from Remy anyway, but Eli heard Ashlyn mutter a soft "no."

There was plenty of emotion in that single word. Especially plenty of fear, because she had to know just how dangerous Remy was right now.

"All right, Eli, we'll deal," Remy finally answered. "Put down your gun and have Gunnar cuff you. I want your hands behind your back. Then you and I will walk out of here and go to the cruiser."

The cuffing wasn't ideal because Eli wouldn't be able to fight back, but he trusted Kellan to stop Remy before they could make it to the cruiser.

Remy's eyes narrowed even more than they already were when he looked at Eli. "If you try to pull anything stupid, I start shooting. The kid could get hurt."

Eli hoped like the devil that Gloria had stayed in the tub with Cora. While he was hoping, he added that they were all right. He could no longer hear the baby crying, so maybe that meant she'd gone back to sleep.

"Here's my gun," Eli said, sliding it across the floor toward Remy. He had a backup, but Remy didn't ask for that.

Remy nodded. "Okay, Gunnar. Get the cuffs on him. And I want to watch you when you do that."

Eli motioned for Gunnar and him to stand, and he went ahead and shot that warning glance at Ashlyn. She was still there in the doorway. Still had a grip on a gun that she had aimed in Remy's direction.

When Eli stood, he eased his hands behind him,

and Gunnar moved closer so he could start putting on the plastic cuffs.

"Remember, no tricks," Remy warned them. "If you pull anything, I shoot, and it wouldn't be my fault. It'd be yours if the kid gets hurt."

Dominick made a deep throaty growl of outrage, and while Eli could understand why the man was furious with Remy's threat, it wasn't a good time for Dominick to be anything but cooperative. Dominick, though, obviously had something different in mind.

Something that could get them all killed.

"This ends now," Dominick spat out, and before the last word had even left his mouth, he whirled around. In the same motion, he took hold of Remy and slung the man across the room.

Remy slammed against Eli, sending them both to the floor.

And Remy pulled the trigger.

Chapter Sixteen

The sound of the shot was deafening, and it was like a blast roaring through Ashlyn's head. She could have sworn she felt the vibration of it all the way to her bones.

She also felt the slam of fear that quickly followed.

Oh God. Had Remy managed to shoot Eli? Or had the bullet gone into the bathroom where Cora was?

She fired glances all around her but didn't see the signs of where any gunshot had landed. However, she did hear Gloria and Cora. Cora was crying, causing Ashlyn's fear to spike even more.

"Cora!" Ashlyn shouted.

"We're okay," Gloria called out. "We're not hurt."

The relief came flooding through her. Her baby hadn't been harmed. The relief was short-lived, though, because Ashlyn knew there could be other shots. Plus, she still wasn't sure if Eli was okay. He certainly wasn't calling out to her to let her know he was all right.

Ashlyn blinked back the tears that automatically started to burn her eyes, and with her gun ready, she hurried out of the doorway of the bedroom and into the hall so she could see what was going on.

And what was going on was chaos.

Eli was alive, thank goodness, but she saw that there was blood on his hands. That tightened the muscles in her chest so that it was hard for her to breathe. The slam of adrenaline didn't help, either. Everything inside her was screaming for her to get to Eli to save him.

But Eli was trying to save himself. He had his hands clamped around Remy's, and the grip no doubt stopped Remy from firing again.

Dominick reached down, scooping up Eli's gun from the floor, and he took aim at Remy.

"No," Gunnar told Dominick, taking the word right out of Ashlyn's mouth. "Don't shoot. You could hit Eli."

Thankfully, Dominick held back, but she could tell from the way he was moving around that he was trying to find a clean shot. Gunnar was doing the same, but Remy wasn't making that easy for them. He and Eli were locked in a fierce battle, rolling around on the floor while Remy kicked and punched at Eli. Somehow, despite all of the blows he was getting, Eli managed to hang on to Remy's shooting hand.

"The fire's out," Kellan said when he hurried in through what was left of the front door. He also had his gun drawn, and he cursed when he saw the struggle that was going on between his brother and Remy.

"Was Remy alone when he brought you here?" Kellan snapped at Dominick.

Dominick nodded and kept moving. Kept looking for that shot. It was obvious he was furious with Remy, and Ashlyn didn't think it was solely because of the kidnapping. She'd heard the rage in Dominick's voice when Remy threatened to fire shots into the house.

Kellan moved to the side of the room, looming near Remy and Eli, and he tipped his head to Dominick. "Move. Go back toward the door and stay down. This clown could get off a shot."

Yes, a shot that could go anywhere, including into Eli or Cora.

"Did you see any other gunmen?" Gunnar asked Kellan.

The question gave her another hit of adrenaline along with another jolt of fear. Eli was in a battle for his life, but she needed to make sure no one tried to climb through the window to get to Cora. Now that Eli had turned off the security system, they wouldn't even know if a hired gun broke in.

Ashlyn hurried back to the doorway, and she volleyed her attention between Eli and the window. Cora had stopped crying again, but it still wasn't easy to hear if someone was approaching the house because of the shouts and curses from the living room.

Even though Ashlyn had tried to steel herself for it, the next shot still stunned her. And put her heart right in her throat. From her position she could partially see Eli, but Kellan was in her way so she couldn't tell if Eli had been hit. Kellan's next round of ripe profanity didn't help that, and he moved in, kicking at something.

Remy's arm, she realized.

Remy howled in pain, and Ashlyn moved out a few inches so she could get a glimpse of Eli. He was still down, and he had Remy's hand pinned to the floor. That didn't stop Remy from pulling the trigger again.

This time, Ashlyn didn't have to guess where the bullet had gone because she saw it blow out a hole in the wall just above Eli's head. Another couple of inches, and he would have been killed.

"Enough of this," Eli snarled.

Ashlyn held her breath and watched as Eli gave Remy's hand another bash on the floor, and then he rammed his elbow into Remy's chest. The man sputtered out a cough, and that split-second lapse was enough for Kellan to move in. He latched onto the back of Remy's shirt collar and dragged him off Eli.

But Remy somehow managed to keep hold of his gun.

A gun that he aimed at Eli.

Ashlyn heard herself yell for Eli to watch out, but he was already scrambling to the side while he reached to draw his backup from his boot holster. He was still reaching for it when the next blast roared through the room.

She froze, her feet seemingly frozen in place, but that didn't stop the horrible thoughts from racing through her head. "Eli," she managed to say. Ashlyn would have gone to him, but Kellan stepped in front of her again.

"You don't need to see this," Kellan said, spiking her fear even more.

Until she realized Eli was fine. Well, he hadn't been shot, anyway. He was on his feet, his backup weapon now in his hand, and he had it pointed at Remy.

Remy wasn't *fine*.

The man was no longer holding his gun. That was good. He was on the floor, his hands pressed to his chest, and Ashlyn had no trouble seeing the blood. It was seeping through his fingers and spilling down the side of his shirt.

"I had to shoot him," Kellan muttered, and it sounded as if he was talking to himself. He went closer and kicked Remy's gun to the other side of the room. "Remy didn't give me a choice about that."

No, he hadn't. Remy's choices had started when he'd taken Dominick hostage and then had come here to the house. Despite Eli trying to reason with him, he'd fired three shots, any of which could have hurt or killed. He had to be stopped, and thankfully Kellan had done it.

"I want to be with Marta," Remy said, his words choppy with his rough breaths. "I want to be buried next to her."

Eli certainly didn't give him any assurances that would happen, and she wondered if Gus would even allow it. Not after everything that Remy had done.

"I'll call for an ambulance." Eli holstered his backup, picked up his gun and then took out his phone to do that, but he also glanced over at Ashlyn. "Is Cora okay?" he asked.

She managed a nod, not trusting her voice. Ashlyn wasn't certain she could speak yet. Not sure she could move to Eli, either, even though that's what she wanted to do. She wanted to hold him, to feel for herself that he was safe. But Eli still had to wrap this up.

"Check on the car and make sure that fire didn't kick back up," Kellan instructed Gunnar.

While Eli continued to hold his gun on Remy, Kellan went to the man, stooped down and pressed his hands over Remy's. Probably to try to slow down the flow of blood. Ashlyn figured that wouldn't help, not with the amount of blood that Remy had already lost.

"Did you hire those guns who tried to kill Ashlyn and Eli?" Kellan asked him.

Remy opened his mouth, maybe to answer, but that's when she heard the rattling sound that came from Remy's throat.

And she watched as Remy died.

Kellan cursed again, probably because a confession would have tied up everything into a neat little bow, but they still might be able to get confirmation from Waite—who was still in custody. Eli had said they could hang charges of accessory to attempted murder over him to get him to talk.

Ashlyn turned to go into the bedroom so she could check on Gloria and Cora, but she'd only made it a step when she felt someone take hold of her shoulder. At first she thought it was Eli, but the grip was too hard. Hard enough to leave bruises. And the person spun her around, knocking her weapon from her hand and dragging her back against his chest.

Dominick put a gun to her head.

ELI'S HEART SLAMMED so hard against his chest that it felt as if he'd cracked a rib. Hell. This couldn't be happening. Not now, after everything they'd just been through.

He dropped down behind the side of the sofa and automatically brought up his gun, taking aim at Dominick. So did Kellan after he took cover behind the end table. But both he and his brother knew that neither of them had a clean shot. Just as they hadn't with Remy when he'd dragged Dominick from the car and into the house. That's because Dominick was now using Ashlyn as a human shield.

Eli couldn't help but see Ashlyn's face and the shock and terror that was on it. He hated that once again she was in danger. As bad as the other attacks had been—and they had been bad—at least the gunmen hadn't managed to get their hands on her. Now Dominick had managed that.

And he'd done it right in front of two armed lawmen.

Eli wanted to kick himself for not seeing what was about to happen. Kick himself, too, for not putting a stop to it. But that led Eli to a couple of questions. Had Dominick ever actually been a hostage, or had this been some kind of sick setup with Remy? Of course, the biggest question on Eli's mind was why Dominick was now holding a gun on Ashlyn.

"Throw down your weapons," Dominick told Eli and Kellan. "Then, listen carefully to what you need to do to keep Ashlyn alive."

Eli forced the muscles in his jaw to ease up so he could speak. "Trust me, I'm listening. Now, what the hell do you want?"

Dominick shook his head and made a sound of frustration. "I wanted things to go a heck of a lot better than this. Since that didn't happen, I'm now on to plan C."

Which meant two other plans had failed. Eli didn't have any trouble filling in the blanks on what Dominick had tried to do.

"You had your own granddaughter kidnapped," Eli started, "and you set me up for that by trying to make Ashlyn believe I was responsible for it. You wanted her to murder me, and once she'd been convicted and was in jail, then you would have had a clear path to get permanent custody of Cora."

Dominick didn't deny anything Eli said, not with words, nor with his expression. This was all about getting his hands on Cora.

Ashlyn's eyes narrowed, and Eli could see her fear and shock replaced for another emotion. Fury. He totally got that. This idiot had put Cora in danger not just by having those thugs kidnap her but also with the attacks.

Of course, Dominick likely thought the baby had never been in danger, but she easily could have been. The hired guns could have turned on Dominick and tried to hold the child for ransom. Cora could have been hurt or worse. And all because Dominick hadn't wanted to "share" her with Ashlyn.

"When Ashlyn didn't take the bait and kill me," Eli went on, "you set your goons on us. Goons who shot us when Cora could have been in the car."

"She wasn't." Dominick's voice took on even a harder edge. "They had orders to make sure she wasn't part of that."

"Orders that you trusted with hired killers," Eli pointed out. "I don't know if that makes you stupid or just plain careless with a child's life."

That sure didn't cool down the fire in Dominick's eyes, and he gave Eli a look that could have frozen hell. "Cora's my granddaughter. My blood kin," he emphasized through clenched teeth. "I will be the one to raise her."

Which meant Dominick was going to have to get Ashlyn out of the way. Along with Kellan and him, too, and any other witnesses.

From the corner of Eli's eye, he saw Kellan move. His brother was shifting his position, trying to get into a better angle to put a stop to this. But Dominick saw it, too, because he immediately turned, keeping Ashlyn in a chokehold in front of him.

"Did you not hear that part about keeping Ashlyn alive?" Dominick snapped. "Trying to shoot me is a surefire way of getting her killed."

Kellan froze. But Eli knew they couldn't just

stand there and let Dominick do whatever he was planning on doing.

Eli listened for any sign that Gunnar was still nearby. He didn't glance outside because he didn't want Dominick to be reminded that the deputy had gone out there. Not that Dominick had forgotten that, but Dominick wasn't a hired killer, and he might not be thinking straight right now. All they needed was some break, a distraction, just enough for Ashlyn to bolt out of Dominick's grip so that Eli could shoot him.

Eli very much wanted to shoot him. And that was a reminder for him to tamp down his anger. That wasn't going to help Ashlyn right now. He needed to keep a clear head.

"Here's how this is going to work," Dominick said. "Ashlyn and I are going to get Cora, and we'll walk out of here. I don't want to use the cruiser that Remy wanted because I suspect there's a tracker on it. Idiot," he grumbled when he glanced at Remy's body.

So that meant Dominick likely hadn't been working with Remy after all. Not that it mattered now, but when they got out of this—and they would—then Eli would want to build a solid case against Dominick. He wanted him in a cage for the rest of his miserable life.

"I'm guessing the reason for this desperation is because you got wind that Waite was about to spill his guts," Eli went on. He wanted to keep Dominick's attention on him so that he didn't notice Gunnar or Kellan. "Waite will confess that you're the one who hired him and his buddy. He must have told you that when you were at the sheriff's office visiting him—right before Remy kidnapped you."

Again, Dominick didn't deny it, but his silence put a cold hard knot in Eli's gut. All along Dominick had been a suspect, but Eli hated that he hadn't gotten the proof sooner. He definitely hadn't wanted things to play out like this what with Ashlyn, Cora, Gloria, Kellan and Gunnar in danger. Plus, some of the hands could get hurt, too, if Dominick tried to escape.

"Your son, Danny, didn't want you to raise Cora," Ashlyn said. "In fact, before he died, he made it clear that he didn't want you anywhere near her."

Dominick tightened his grip on Ashlyn's neck, and Eli could feel the man's anger go up a notch. Obviously, this was a sensitive subject, and while Eli wouldn't have minded pushing some of Dominick's buttons, he didn't want to do that while he was holding a gun on Ashlyn.

"My son was on drugs and confused," Dominick spat out. "If he'd been thinking straight, he would have made sure that she wasn't put up for adoption where anyone could have ended up getting her. She's my granddaughter, and with Danny dead, she belongs to me."

In his own way, Dominick was just as crazy and obsessed as Remy had been. That only made him more dangerous, because there was no way to reason with someone this bent on getting his way.

"Cora belongs to me," Ashlyn snapped, and she was just as angry as Dominick. Definitely not good. Eli didn't want her to do anything that would goad the man into pulling the trigger.

"Until you can prove to me that she has your DNA, then she's mine." This time Dominick dug the gun even harder into her head just as Remy had done to him minutes earlier.

"Both of you want what's best for Cora," Eli interjected, trying to get Dominick to turn back to him. "Just make sure you don't fire any shots that can go through the walls."

That did get Dominick's attention, and he finally turned his glare back on Eli. "If I shoot, I won't be aiming at a wall."

No. He'd be shooting at Ashlyn, and she'd be a very easy target. But for now, Dominick almost certainly wanted to keep her alive because he thought she was his ticket out of there. With his money and resources, he no doubt planned to take the baby, murder Ashlyn, and then he'd disappear with Cora.

Eli didn't intend for any of that to happen.

"I need a vehicle," Dominick reminded them. "I'll take the keys to your truck." He meant that for Eli. "First, put your gun on the floor. You, too,

Sheriff Slater. And before the two of you think of delaying that some more, just know that I will shoot. Nowhere near where Cora is, but that end table isn't giving the sheriff much protection. I'm thinking a bullet could go through that without a problem."

It could, and Eli wasn't immune to the threat of having his brother shot. Or of having any gunfire. There'd already been enough bloodshed. But Eli also had no intention of facing Dominick while he was unarmed.

Eli slid his gun across the floor toward Dominick, and in the same motion, he drew his backup from his boot holster. He kept that out of sight. From behind the table, Kellan did the same, drawing his backup as well.

"Good," Dominick continued. "Now, go ahead and take your keys from your pocket and slide them over here. Remember not to do anything that'll get your lover killed. That includes giving me the wrong key and trying to charge at me when I reach down for them."

Eli doubted that Dominick had any proof that Ashlyn and he were indeed lovers, but it was possible they were giving off some kind of vibe. Eli knew he wasn't reining in all his emotions when he looked at her, but he didn't want Dominick using that in some way.

He took out his keys and as instructed, Eli slid them toward Dominick. They stopped just a few inches from his feet. Dominick tightened his hold on Ashlyn even more, causing her to make a gasping sound. A sound that made Eli want to do that charging that Dominick had already warned him about.

Eli moved back behind the sofa and waited for any chance he had to put a stop to this.

Dominick stooped down, dragging Ashlyn with him. "Pick up the keys," he told her.

She did, closing her fingers around them, and when her gaze met Eli's, he wanted to curse. Because he could tell that Ashlyn was about to make a move. A move that he prayed wouldn't get her killed.

Before Dominick had fully stood back up, Ashlyn turned, ramming the keys into his face. The metal gouged his cheek, causing him to shout out in pain, and he cursed her, calling her a vile name. However, the injury wasn't enough for him to break the hold he had on Ashlyn. He yanked her, hard, against him, and this time she did more than gasp.

Dominick was choking her.

"Gloria?" Dominick called out. "I know you're back there, and you have Cora with you. Bring her out to me now, or Ashlyn dies."

Chapter Seventeen

Ashlyn prayed that Gloria would stay put in the bathroom. She started to shout to the sitter to do just that, but the chokehold Dominick had on her was so tight now that she couldn't speak.

Couldn't breathe.

Plus, Dominick had threatened to shoot Kellan. And she was certain the man would do just that. In fact, he'd be looking for any excuse right now to eliminate the lawmen in the room, because that would give him a clearer path to killing Gloria and her. That had to be his end goal, to get them all out of the way so he could walk out with Cora.

It sickened Ashlyn to think that his plan could possibly work. No way was anyone going to risk firing shots at Dominick if he had the baby in his arms. Then, once he had Cora in Eli's truck, he could simply disappear.

Even if she managed to stay alive, Ashlyn might not ever find her baby. That's why she had to stop

Dominick now. It didn't matter if Cora and he had DNA in common. She was Cora's mother, and Dominick was a monster and had no right to take her.

She clawed at Dominick's hands until he finally eased up on his grip. By the time he did that, Ashlyn's lungs were aching, and she gulped in several quick breaths, causing herself to cough. However, she did manage to hold on to the keys, and she hoped she got a chance to use them again. She poked the largest key through her fingers, turning it into a weapon, but she also kept it down by her side so that Dominick hopefully wouldn't see what she'd done.

"Gloria?" Dominick yelled again. "I start shooting if you don't come out here now with Cora."

Again, Gloria didn't answer, but Ashlyn was positive the sitter had heard the threat and was no doubt debating what to do. Ashlyn was doing the same, and maybe Gloria would just stay put until Eli, Kellan or she could stop Dominick.

Or maybe Gunnar could.

Ashlyn had been glancing outside but hadn't spotted the deputy in the last five minutes or so. Certainly, Gunnar had heard what was going on and had hopefully called for backup. Or else he was waiting and trying to work out a way to get inside and sneak up on him.

She didn't think Dominick had brought any hired guns with him. If he had, he would have already used them. So that meant Gunnar wasn't likely to be ambushed. That was something, at least. But she had to wonder if Dominick was working alone in this.

"Did you team up with Oscar or Remy?" she managed to ask, though it was still hard to talk with his tight grip on her neck.

Dominick made a quick sound of surprise. Or maybe disgust. "No. Both are idiots."

So Remy's kidnapping had been just that. A kidnapping that'd stemmed from desperation.

"Oscar might be useful, though, if I can set him up for this," Dominick added in a mumble.

Ashlyn hoped it didn't come down to that. Because if it did, it would mean she, Kellan, Eli and Gunnar would be dead. So would any of the hands who'd witnessed any of this.

"Tell Gloria to come out," Dominick snapped to Ashlyn. "Tell her Eli will die if she doesn't. I can put a bullet through that couch and straight into him. He'll die because of you. Do you really want to see someone you love die right in front you again?"

No. She didn't. In fact, just mentioning that triggered some flashbacks that she had to force away. She couldn't let that play into this now. She had to keep her focus. Ashlyn shook her head, not sure of what she should do, but Eli spoke before she could figure it out.

"Let Dominick shoot me," Eli said, his voice calm and hard at the same time. "That means he'll have to take the gun off you, and when he does, Gunnar will kill him with a shot to the head."

Ashlyn felt the muscles tense in Dominick's arm and chest, and even though she couldn't see his face, she thought maybe his gaze was firing all around.

"Yeah," Eli added. "Gunnar's got sniper skills, and he's got a gun aimed at you right now. All he's doing is waiting for you to move. An inch is all he needs to end your worthless life."

"You're lying," Dominick spat out, but he didn't sound as if he was so certain of that.

Neither was Ashlyn. She knew it could be a bluff, but Gunnar was indeed out there somewhere, so it was highly likely that he had Dominick in his sights.

"You really think I'm lying?" Eli taunted. He kept his gaze nailed to Dominick. "If you honestly believe that, then you should be checking out the window to see for yourself who's watching you."

Ashlyn saw Eli shift a little, leaning out from the sofa as if daring Dominick to take aim at him. That caused her heart to jump to her throat. She didn't want Eli putting himself in the line of fire like this. She definitely didn't want him hurt or dead because he was protecting Cora and her.

Again, she felt Dominick tense, and maybe he did glance outside. If so, it wasn't for long, and he didn't shift his position enough because Eli stayed put. He didn't get that shot that he was no doubt hoping for.

"Ashlyn and I will go and get Cora," Dominick finally growled. "Tell your deputy friend that he'd better back off."

Neither Eli nor Kellan did that, and she saw both of them move again when Dominick started down the hall with her. He kept her in a chokehold and took slow, cautious steps backward. He was almost certainly glancing behind him as well as keeping an eye on Kellan and Eli.

It didn't take long, only a few steps, before Ashlyn lost sight of Eli. Kellan was still there, though, but that was because he inched to the side of the table. That's when Ashlyn noticed the gun he was holding. His backup weapon, no doubt. Good. He had a way to fight back if it came down to that.

Even with the porch light still on, it was hard for her to see in the yard, but she searched through the darkness to try to spot Gunnar. Still no sign of him, but she heard movement. Apparently, so did Dominick, because he stopped.

"Just remember that at any time, I can put a bullet in Ashlyn," Dominick called out as a warning. "It won't kill her, but she'll be in a lot of pain, and it'll all be your fault."

No, it wouldn't be. The blame for this was solely on Dominick, but Ashlyn doubted anyone would convince him of that.

Dominick stayed still several more seconds. Clearly, he was listening, but Ashlyn was thankful what he wasn't hearing were any sounds coming from the bathroom. Cora wasn't crying, and Gloria was keeping quiet. Of course, that might change once they made it to the door, and she figured that wouldn't take much time. There wasn't much space between the hall and that bathroom.

"Don't do anything stupid," Dominick warned her again, and he started moving. Walking backward until they made it to the doorway of the bedroom.

Ashlyn glanced inside and didn't see anyone, but there was light spilling from beneath the bathroom door. She also noticed that the room seemed warmer than the rest of the house. For one terrifying moment she thought maybe the fire from the car had spread back here, but the fire wasn't spreading. Plus, it wasn't that kind of heat. It was just the humid hot air from the night.

And that's when she noticed the bedroom window.

It was open, causing the curtains to flutter in the breeze. Since it had been closed before this whole ordeal had started, it meant Gunnar had likely opened it. Maybe so he could get inside, or he could have done it to give himself a better shot.

Dominick stopped, and he cursed when he saw the window. That sent him snapping in all directions, dragging her along with each move he made. He shifted his gun, taking aim at each corner of the room, but if someone was there, they were staying out of sight.

"I'll kill her if you make it necessary," Dominick spat out, speaking to no one in particular.

His breathing was a lot faster now, practically gusting, and Ashlyn could feel his heart thudding against her back. She didn't mind if he was scared, but she didn't want him to panic and do something dangerous that could get Cora hurt.

She heard someone moving around in the living room. Kellan and Eli no doubt. The only way they could access the bedroom from inside the house was to come down the hall. A hall that Dominick was still clearly watching. But if either Eli or Kellan went outside, they could come in through the open window.

Dominick kept moving, inching his way to the bathroom door, and when he reached it, he used his foot to knock. "Open up, Gloria!" he shouted.

No answer.

Ashlyn tried to tamp down her own pulse so she could hear any sounds of her baby, but nothing. That didn't help with the fear that was already skyrocketing. Mercy, had something happened?

"Gloria?" Dominick banged his foot even harder against the door, but he stopped abruptly and pivoted her in the direction of the hall. Adjusting her so that she was squarely in front of him. And Ashlyn soon saw why.

Eli.

He was no longer by the sofa but was peering

out from the wall that led into the hall. He was close, but he still wouldn't have a clean shot. Not with Dominick's position. If Eli missed, the bullet could go through the door and into the bathroom.

"Gloria!" Dominick shouted, and she could feel the rage bubbling inside him. He was quickly losing control.

She adjusted the grip on the keys, getting ready to make her move. Ashlyn figured she wouldn't be able to go for his face this time, but she would jam the keys like a knife in his thigh. If that was enough to break the hold he had on her, then she could drop to the floor and hopefully drag him down with her.

Dominick's next shout for Gloria was even louder, and without warning he turned and bashed his body against the door. Again and again. Harder and harder.

Until the door flew open.

Dominick pivoted to the side, no doubt looking around the small room, just as Ashlyn was doing. And what she saw caused her heartbeat to go into overdrive.

The bathtub was empty.

Neither Gloria nor Cora was there, and there wasn't any place in the room for them to hide. They were simply gone, and not knowing where they were or what happened to them nearly sent Ashlyn into a panic.

Dominick cursed, his words vile and raw, and his

profanity only got worse when his attention landed on the open bathroom window. But Ashlyn wasn't cursing. The relief came because she knew that Gloria had managed to escape. Maybe with help from Gunnar. If so, she prayed that Gunnar had them tucked somewhere safe. Away from Dominick and any shots he might fire.

"Call out for Gloria," Dominick demanded, strangling her again. "Tell her to bring Cora in here right now!"

Even if Ashlyn could have spoken at that moment, she wouldn't have done that. Not even if Dominick threatened to kill her again. No way would she do anything to bring her baby back into the middle of this.

Since the strangling was blurring her vision, Ashlyn figured she didn't have long before she passed out. That meant she had to do something now, especially since Dominick was already dragging her toward the window—maybe so he could take her outside to look for Cora.

Ashlyn pinpointed all her strength into her hand, and she rammed the keys into the side of his leg. Dominick howled in pain, cursing her again, but he also staggered back. It was just enough for him to move the gun away from her head. Also enough for him to ease up on the chokehold. Ashlyn took advantage of that and dropped to the floor.

Even though she was gasping for air and her

throat was throbbing, she swung out at him again with the keys, digging them into his other leg. As he roared with pain, their eyes met, and in that instant she saw that rage had tightened all the muscles in his face. There was pure hatred in his eyes. And she also saw something else.

That he was about to shoot her.

Dominick shifted, taking aim with his gun to do just that, and she knew at that range, he wouldn't miss.

The blast came, thick and loud. It echoed through the room. Through her head. And it was followed by a second shot, one just as loud as the first.

Ashlyn braced herself for the pain. But it didn't come. It took her a moment to realize that she hadn't been shot.

But Eli had been.

Eli was in the doorway of the bathroom, and there was blood on his shirt. God. *Blood*. But despite that, he still had his gun aimed at Dominick. He was bleeding, too, and it was spreading across the front of his shirt. Eli and he had exchanged shots, and both had been hit.

Groaning, Dominick turned and jumped out the window.

Escaping.

Eli took aim again, but it was too late. Dominick was gone.

Chapter Eighteen

Eli felt the burning and the pain in his arm and knew he'd been shot. Despite that, plenty of things had just gone right. Ashlyn hadn't been hurt, and Dominick hadn't managed to get to the baby.

Now Eli had to make sure things stayed that way, along with catching Dominick and making sure he paid for all the things he'd done. Things that could have left all of them dead and Cora in the hands of a killer.

"Cora!" Ashlyn practically shouted.

Despite the alarm on her face when she looked at his bloody shirtsleeve, she scrambled away from him to get to the window. No doubt because she thought that Cora and Gloria were out there where Dominick could still get to them.

Eli hurried to her, took hold of her and pulled her from the window. He also slapped off the lights so that Dominick wouldn't be able to see them.

And shoot them.

Because while Cora and Gloria weren't out in the yard, Dominick was.

"Gunnar has Cora and Gloria," Eli told Ashlyn, and even though she was still struggling to get away from him, he maneuvered her out of the bathroom and back into the hall where they wouldn't be in Dominick's line of sight.

It obviously took several seconds for his words to sink in, but Ashlyn finally stopped trying to fight him off, and blinking, she stared up at him. "Cora's all right?"

Eli nodded. "Gunnar texted me about five minutes ago. He went in through the bathroom window, got Gloria and the baby out, and took them to the cruiser. It's bullet-resistant," he reminded her. "Gloria has the baby on the floor of the car so Dominick can't see them. The hands are guarding them to make sure Dominick doesn't get close."

Her breath swooshed out, and she practically sagged against him. "Cora's all right," she said. "My baby's all right."

But her relief was very short-lived. Almost immediately, the alarm returned to her eyes, and Ashlyn's gaze slashed to his shirtsleeve.

"Oh God. You've been shot," she blurted out. "Dominick shot you."

"It's okay. *I'm* okay." Though Eli thought it was more than just a scratch, he had no intention of telling Ashlyn that. Not when she was so close to panicking.

Ashlyn volleyed her attention between his face and the wound, and she shook her head. "How soon can an ambulance get here?" So, she wasn't buying his *I'm okay*, and she eased up his sleeve to take a look.

"Soon. Kellan called for one, but it won't be able to get on the grounds until we're sure it's safe."

"Safe," Ashlyn repeated. "You mean not until Dominick is caught." She paused, her bottom lip trembling a little. Considering everything she'd just been through, that was a fairly mild reaction. However, he was betting that every nerve in her body was rattled right now. "You shot him."

Eli nodded. Then he silently cursed himself. "I should have gotten off a second shot so he couldn't get away. I should have killed him."

Apparently, Ashlyn wasn't the only one with rattled nerves, but it had cut him to the bone to see Dominick holding that gun to her head and hearing the man threaten to take Cora. It had also cleared Eli's mind in a very unexpected way. The fear had cut through the old wounds, their pasts, and it had made him realize just how much Ashlyn and Cora meant to him.

They meant everything to him.

Everything.

"You need an ambulance, and I need to see Cora," Ashlyn said, shifting his attention back to her. Not that it had strayed too far away, but Eli was keeping watch to make sure Dominick didn't try to get back in the house.

"Soon," Eli assured her.

Because he thought they could both use it, he brushed a kiss on her cheek. That's when he noticed the bruises already forming on her temple and throat. Both were reminders of what Dominick had done to her. That caused a whole new round of anger to slam through him.

"How soon will the ambulance be here?" she pressed, and Ashlyn ripped off part of his sleeve to form a makeshift tourniquet on his arm.

"After Kellan and the hands find Dominick and arrest him."

She looked up at him, and he saw her blink back tears. "They have to find him, Eli."

Yeah, they did. And while Eli was certain that would happen, he also knew that Ashlyn and he wouldn't be breathing easier until the man was in custody. As long as Dominick was out there, he could manage to escape and get away from the ranch. Maybe even get help and recover from his gunshot wound, and that meant he could try to come after Ashlyn and Cora again.

That sent a new round of anger through Eli. Ashlyn and Cora had been through enough, and he didn't want them having to live out their lives while keeping watch for a snake like Dominick.

"The danger has to end," Ashlyn said, her voice

more breath than sound, and she put her arms around him, pulling him close to her.

He didn't have any trouble making the contact even tighter. He looped his good arm around her, and this time when he kissed her, it wasn't on her cheek. He really kissed her, pouring all his anger and relief into it. It helped. Well, it helped him, but it caused his wound to throb. That didn't make him let go. Just holding her like this gave him another of those realizations like the one he'd gotten when Dominick had her hostage.

Eli wanted Ashlyn and Cora in his life.

He was about to tell her that when his phone dinged with a text. "It's from Kellan," he told Ashlyn, and he read through the message. "No sign of Dominick yet, but Gunnar's going to pull the cruiser right up to the door. Kellan wants you and me to get in it. Then Gunnar can get us out of here."

Eli didn't add that his brother was concerned about Dominick trying to double back and sneak into the house. Best not to put that idea in Ashlyn's head, especially when she already had enough bad memories and nightmare images there.

"I can see Cora," Ashlyn muttered. "And if there's a first aid kit in the cruiser, I can take care of your arm until you can see an EMT."

There was that, and Eli wanted to be closer to Cora so he could make sure she was safe. But Eli also knew this meant having Ashlyn go out into the open. Even if it would only be for a few seconds, it was still a risk. A risk that Kellan must have thought was worth taking. Maybe because Dominick was still close to the house?

Hell.

Eli hoped not, but if so, he would have to stay on guard and be ready. He watched as the cruiser drove up, moving as close to the house as the driver could get. The ranch hands hurried to flank the car, one on all four sides, and each of them was armed.

"Move fast," Eli told her.

Though the reminder wasn't necessary. The moment the front passenger's door opened, she took hold of Eli and started running. Ashlyn scrambled in first, moving to the middle of the seat next to Gunnar, who was behind the wheel. Eli got in right after Ashlyn.

The first thing Eli heard was Cora. The baby was making cooing sounds, and when he looked in the back seat, he saw the baby smiling as Gloria talked to her. Thank goodness Cora wasn't scared—though Eli could see plenty of fear on Gloria's face. However, there was relief on Ashlyn's.

Ashlyn, too, was smiling when she leaned over the seat to kiss the baby, and Eli found himself smiling right along with them. Yeah, he definitely wanted them in his life and would figure out a way to make that happen as soon as they were all safe.

"The ambulance is just up the road," Gunnar explained. He glanced at the blood on Eli's arm and frowned. "Sorry that happened."

Eli shook his head. "It's nothing. Thanks for getting Gloria and Cora out of the house."

"Yes, thank you," Ashlyn echoed.

She was still leaning over the seat when Eli heard something else. Something he didn't want to hear.

"Watch out!" someone shouted. Kellan. "He's coming your way!"

Eli pivoted to the sound of his brother's voice, but instead of seeing Kellan, he spotted Dominick. The man was coming out of the house and running straight toward them. Kellan was on the side of the house. Also running. But he might not be able to intercept Dominick in time.

"Get down now," Eli ordered, and he hoped that Ashlyn and Gloria would listen.

Dominick was a mess with blood all over the front of his shirt, and he was staggering, but he still had a gun. A gun that he had pointed at the cruiser. Even though there was little chance a bullet would be able to get through, Eli didn't take any chances. Barreling out of the cruiser, he took aim.

And fired.

This time, he didn't hold back. He sent three shots straight into Dominick's chest. There was a startled look on Dominick's face as if he couldn't believe what'd just happened, but the look was gone in a flash. His expression went blank, and Dominick collapsed onto the ground.

Dead.

Eli was sure of that, but he kept his gun on the man as he hurried to him. He kicked away Dominick's gun, leaned down and touched his fingers to his neck. He was definitely gone.

"Sorry," Kellan said, running in behind Eli. "I spotted Dominick, but he got away from me. I didn't want to shoot because I wasn't sure if Ashlyn and you were still in the house."

Kellan stopped and cursed when he saw the blood on Eli. "Let me get the EMTs up here for you."

Eli didn't stop him from doing that, but right now his injury wasn't his main concern. Ashlyn was. She had no doubt watched as he'd gunned down Dominick, and Eli had to confirm she was okay.

He made sure he didn't wince in pain when he made his way back to her. Ashlyn must have sensed it, though, because she got out of the cruiser, and she forced him to sit on the seat.

"It's over," she said, not sounding as shaky as he'd thought she would. She stepped closer, standing between his legs and looking down at him. "Thank you."

He didn't want her thanks. Didn't deserve it. Because he hadn't stopped the danger that'd led them to this.

"I should have seen how unhinged Dominick was," he told her.

The look she gave him turned a little flat. "I think Dominick hid it well. Until tonight, that is. But he'll never be able to come after us again."

True, and neither would Waite. Not that Eli thought Waite was a threat now. Not with Dominick's money fueling him. Still, Eli wanted him to pay, too.

In the distance, he heard the sirens from the ambulance. It wouldn't be long before it arrived, and he couldn't see how he was going to talk Ashlyn and Kellan out of making him go to the hospital. Besides, he was pretty sure he needed stitches, and he'd need to be examined if only to stop Ashlyn from worrying about him.

"When you told me you were in love with me," he started, "I dismissed it."

She gave a heavy sigh. "It's okay. I understand."

That made him frown. "Well, you shouldn't understand, because I had no right to dismiss it. Not when I feel the same way about you."

He'd said those last words fast, just to make sure he got them all out before the ambulance got there. And even though he was certain that Ashlyn heard him, she didn't have the response he wanted.

She gave him another flat look. One that went on for several too-long moments. And then Ashlyn smiled.

"You're in love with me?" she asked.

Gunnar cleared his throat, obviously trying to remind him he was there, listening. Eli didn't care. He had a sudden, unexplainable urge to shout it from the rooftops, and he might just do that after he got stitched up. And after he kissed Ashlyn.

"I do love you," Eli told her, and he got busy with the kiss.

Eli pulled her down to him, easing her into his lap so he could do it the right way. He kissed her long and deep, and he didn't stop, not even when the ambulance pulled into the yard. He just kept kissing her until what he felt for her washed away some of the ugliness of the night. Heck, it was the cure for a lot of things, because he felt a whole lot better.

Ashlyn gave "better" a notch up. "Good. Because I'm still very much in love with you."

Their gazes connected, and they shared another smile. Another kiss. Eli hadn't thought there could be any more notching up, but he was wrong. Ashlyn took Cora when Gloria handed her to Ashlyn, and suddenly Eli had a beautiful, smiling baby in both their arms.

"Cora and I are a package deal," Ashlyn reminded him.

Eli didn't have to think how he felt about that. He knew. He gathered both Ashlyn and Cora close and kissed them both. Because this was one package deal that made everything perfect.

* * * * *

Look for the final book in
USA TODAY *bestselling author*
Delores Fossen's
Longview Ridge Ranch miniseries when
His Brand of Justice *goes on sale next month!*

And don't miss any of the
previous books in the series:

Safety Breach
A Threat to His Family

Available now wherever
Harlequin Intrigue books are sold!

WE HOPE YOU ENJOYED
THIS BOOK FROM
HARLEQUIN
INTRIGUE

Seek thrills. Solve crimes. Justice served.

Dive into action-packed stories that will keep you
on the edge of your seat. Solve the crime
and deliver justice at all costs.

6 NEW BOOKS AVAILABLE EVERY MONTH!

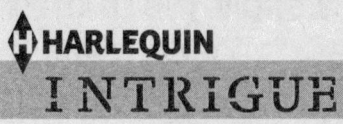
#1947 CONARD COUNTY: HARD PROOF
Conard County: The Next Generation • by Rachel Lee
Former soldier and newbie deputy Candela "Candy" Serrano is assigned
as a liaison to Steve Hawks, the host of TV's *Ghostly Encounters*. Chasing
shadows isn't Candy's idea of police work, but soon some very real killings
start occuring around town...

#1948 HIS BRAND OF JUSTICE
Longview Ridge Ranch • by Delores Fossen
The only person who knows who killed Marshal Jack Slater's father is
Caroline Moser. But the Texas profiler has no memory of the murder, her
abduction...or Jack. Now in Jack's protective custody, Caroline must trust
her ex to help her recall her past before a murderer steals their future.

#1949 PROTECTIVE ORDER
A Badge of Honor Mystery • by Rita Herron
Reese Taggart's search for her sister's stalker lands her in Whistler, NC,
where she must win the trust of arson investigator Griff Maverick. But as the
pair close in on the criminal, can Griff stop Reese from using herself as bait?

#1950 BURIED SECRETS
Holding the Line • by Carol Ericson
To halt construction of a casino on Yaqui land, ranger Jolene Nighthawk
plants damning evidence. But she's caught by her ex, Border Patrol agent
Sam Cross. As Jolene and Sam investigate a series of deaths, they find that
their bodies may be the next ones hidden in Arizona sand.

#1951 LAST STAND SHERIFF
Winding Road Redemption • by Tyler Anne Snell
Soon after Remi Hudson tells Sheriff Declan Nash he's going to be a dad,
Remi becomes the target of repeated attacks. Declan will do anything to
keep her and their unborn baby safe, especially once he realizes the danger
is related to an unsolved case involving his family.

#1952 CAUGHT IN THE CROSSFIRE
Blackhawk Security • by Nichole Severn
When Kate Monroe's deceased husband suddenly appears, the profiler
can't believe her eyes. Declan Monroe has lost all of his memories, but
with a killer targeting Kate, the pair will have to work together to outwit the
Hunter...and find their way back to each other.

Get 4 FREE REWARDS!

We'll send you 2 FREE Books plus 2 FREE Mystery Gifts.

Harlequin Intrigue books are action-packed stories that will keep you on the edge of your seat. Solve the crime and deliver justice at all costs.

FREE Value Over $20

Love Harlequin romance?

DISCOVER.

Be the first to find out about promotions,
news and exclusive content!

f Facebook.com/HarlequinBooks

y Twitter.com/HarlequinBooks

◉ Instagram.com/HarlequinBooks

℗ Pinterest.com/HarlequinBooks

ReaderService.com

EXPLORE.

Sign up for the Harlequin e-newsletter and
download a free book from any series at
TryHarlequin.com

CONNECT.

Join our Harlequin community to
share your thoughts and connect
with other romance readers!
Facebook.com/groups/HarlequinConnection

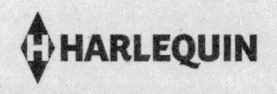

HSOCIAL2020